ADORA CROOKS

THE ROYAL'S LOVE · BOOK 2

THE
ROYAL'S
BABY

* * *

Subscribe to my newsletter for a free short story!

1

RORY

I'm minding my own business at the bar, picking through a plate of a German egg pasta called *spätzle*, when the insults start flying.

My German is rusty at best, but I know enough to make out the sneered words: "Ack! Turn it off—I won't listen to that sick freak!"

I turn my eyes up to the television hanging crookedly in the corner. The local news is playing an interview with Roland Pennington, prince of England. Just the sight of him makes my pulse beat a little faster—it's so strange, seeing him the way other people see him, on TV like this. The camera loves him, and it's not hard to see why—his dashing smile, his twinkling blue eyes, his golden mane of hair. *My lion.*

The interviewer loves him, England loves him, and *I* love him. But the two German men circling the pool table in this Berlin dive bar have a different opinion, and they aren't afraid to show it.

"Shut that pervert up!"

"*Schwuchtel!*"

"Where's his American slut, eh?"

They spit and snarl, clearly having no idea that the *Amer-*

1

ican slut they're referring to is sitting barely three feet away from them, with a meal that's suddenly gone sour.

We knew we would get backlash, coming out like we did. It's been over a year now since Roland announced to the world that he has not one, but two loves in his life: Ben, his best friend and loyal then-bodyguard, and me, the American tourist who stumbled into a love story as beautiful as it is bizarre. England was supposed to be just one more stop on my way to see the world for my brother who couldn't; I'd go to new countries, take videos, and send them home to Oscar, who was stuck at home with a crippling illness. Instead of a good story, I met Roland and Ben, and the three of us fell in love. It shouldn't work, but somehow, some way, it does.

I love my two men—Prince Roland, who has so much energy, compassion, and love in him that sometimes it overwhelms me. And Ben, our quiet, sometime surly lover whose loyalty knows no bounds and who can make my body hum just by putting his hands on my throat. We've overcome insane odds and grown together. In our world, in our little bubble, it's perfect.

But as soon as I step outside Helmsway Palace (as I do, often—these traveling legs won't sit still), I remember the cold truth: that the rest of the world is still struggling to understand our love.

And some—like the two men behind me—have turned their confusion to hate.

I pinch my bottom lip between my teeth. I know I should stay out of it. I'm the prince of England's girlfriend now, which means certain things are *expected* of me. I'm no longer allowed to wear ripped jeans and Doc Martens 24/7. I have to watch my mouth and can no longer swear like a sailor on my (increasingly popular) travel vlog. And I'm *definitely* not supposed to engage with drunken, homophobic Germans who can't wrap their small heads around love is love *is love*.

Buuuut…

2

Your girl Rory March has never been incredibly good at following the rules.

I pay my bill, push away from the bar, and step over to the pool table. I can feel eyes on me—that would be Sam, my bodyguard, watching me from behind her Shirley Temple a couple of seats over. Traveling on my own is one thing I would never—could never—give up, so I've since made concessions to appease my overly protective boyfriends: Sam is one, and my multitude of disguises is another. Right now, for example, I'm wearing a black wig that stops short at my shoulders to conceal my trademark ginger hair. Between the wig and a black romper that is comfortable, casual, and cute, I can tell that the men at the pool table still don't recognize me even when I'm right up next to them. I motion to the table, and in my American-accented, bad German I ask sweetly, "Do you mind if I play, too?"

They exchange looks, then one grins leeringly and passes me his cue. We establish that I'm stripes, his partner is solids. The man I'm playing against is a burly, built guy, and the muscles that flex in his arms when he arranges himself over the pool table briefly remind me of my Ben, my wolf, and the hard biceps that stretch when he pins my wrists effortlessly above my head. It's been a *while*, too long, and I fidget with a present that remind me of my boys—a necklace that hugs my throat with a small cat figure on the end of it. *Their kitten.* It's a pet name they gave me when we were first dating, and it stuck. And, boy, can my men make me purr...

My daydreams scatter as the pool balls click together. My opponent stands and turns to me, smugly, and says in stilted English, "Your turn, darling."

I retract my previous thought—he looks nothing like Ben. Similar builds, maybe, but Ben's dark eyes are full of aching love and compassion. This man's face, though handsome at first glance, is ugly with lines of anger and superiority etched into his jack-o'-lantern mouth and *anything-you-can-do-I-can-do-better* eyes.

What he *doesn't* know is that during Prince Roland's decade of isolation in the palace, he became very good at two-person games—darts, chess, and yes, pool. As a result, I went from not knowing which end of the stick to hit the balls with to becoming *pretty damn good*, if I do say so myself, after multiple games of what we called *strip pool*. We also left a couple of unsightly stains on the pool table, which…sorry to the maid who had to clean up after us. Really. Sorry.

I bend over the pool table, relax my grip on the cue, and line up my shot. I can almost feel Roland's hands teasing my hips, his breath on my neck, his cocky smile on my throat: *Sorry, am I distracting you?*

Yeah, babe, you are.

I exhale a breath, steady my focus, and tap the ball. The cue hits with just the right force and I sink a ball in the hole. And another, and another. We go a few rounds back and forth—my opponent's smile drops, he talks less, and when he does say something, it's in a German mutter I don't understand. The whole game doesn't last ten minutes before I sink my final ball in.

"Well," I say cheerily as I pass the cue over. "Not so bad for an *American slut*, am I?"

I linger just long enough to see the recognition dawn on their faces as their mouths fall open. On my way out the door, the second German—the bigger one—starts after me with a single, growled "Hey!"

But my bodyguard, Sam—all five foot one of cucumber cool—is already between us, and she peels back her black blazer just enough, I know, to reveal the firearm holstered at her side. "I wouldn't," she warns him.

The threat is enough to stop him in his tracks. Meanwhile, Sam and I make a swift exit out into the street.

It's late December and Berlin is freezing. The entire city

is covered in a coat of white snow. I've got a parka with me, and I pull it over my shoulders as the wind bites my cheeks. The chill or the dark of nighttime sobers me up, and we walk past buildings covered in surreal, post-war graffiti. I heave a sigh and see my breath crystalize in front of me.

"I'm sorry," I say to Sam. "I know I forced you to Hulk out, and I shouldn't have—"

"You absolutely *should* have," Sam insists. "Please—they were being complete pricks. Badass bitches like us have got to put little boys in their places sometimes."

And *this* is why I love Sam. I thought it would suck not having Ben as my personal bodyguard—and there are late nights when it *does*—but then there are moments like this. I grew up with a brother, and now I have not one, but *two* boyfriends; Sam is the female empowering *attagirl* that I need on my shoulder. My sister from a British mister. Ben hand-picked her himself, which is all I need to know about the strength of her credentials, but I don't think even he realized what a source of gal-pal comfort she'd be to me.

Or maybe he did. My boyfriends have a way of knowing what I need most—even when I don't know it myself.

"I only wish he'd put up more of a fight," Sam huffs. "Would've liked an excuse to break his nose."

I hook my arm in hers. "Since I failed to provide you a good bar fight," I tell her, "how about a minibar nightcap?"

"It won't make up, but it's a start."

We laugh and Sam hails a car to our hotel.

* * *

I'M STAYING at Hotel Adlon Kempinski—another one of my concessions to Ben and Roland's rampant paranoia. It's hard to believe that, not so long ago, I was backpacking across the world, hopping from hostel to hostel and cataloging my experiences on my vlog, *March On!* (a play on our names,

Oscar and Rory March). My adventures started after my older brother, Oscar, was diagnosed with cystic fibrosis, a condition that left him wheelchair-bound and incapable of leaving the house, let alone the country. So I traveled for him. I went from country to country, getting lost, making friends, and most importantly, documenting everything for my brother so he could see the world through my eyes.

I still travel, but things are different now. Instead of a hostel, I'm granted access to five-star hotels all across the world. It's the kind of luxury I couldn't care less about; I'll take the community of hostel life over a high thread count any day. But I have to take certain security measures as the girlfriend of royalty. There *are* some perks to a pampered life...the hotel minibar, for example, is a nice touch. Even though I can't touch it. I haven't been able to for weeks. Still, *someone* should take advantage of it, so I tell Sam to help herself as I go to the bathroom to change into sweatpants and a loose shirt.

My black wig lies like a dead animal on the sink. As I'm taking the pins out of my hair, my phone starts to ring. It's a video request, and when I see the caller ID, I grin and answer it.

"Bonjovi, Otter," I say as I prop the phone up on the sink.

"Bonjovi," my brother responds. Oscar—or "Otter" as I've affectionately nicknamed him—looks good, his ginger hair tamed and slicked back. He's not wearing his nasal cannula— the at-home tube that attaches his nose and pumps oxygen through him—which is a good sign. The new drugs he's taking have been working wonders, and each small improvement thrills me to no end. "Where in the world is Carmen Sandiego?"

"Berlin, for now. But I'm leaving in the morning. *What* in the world is my brother wearing?"

"Oh, this?" He glances down at the ugly Christmas sweater, which features a Rudolph in the middle and red-

6

nose pom-poms scattered around him. "Francesca is taking me to her Christmas office party."

"Oh! Is she there? Can I say hi?"

He shakes his head. "She's swinging by in a few to pick me up."

"She's taking you to her office party, huh? As her *boyfriend?*" I stretch out the word. "Sounds serious."

"You know what else is serious?" he says, trying to not-so-casually steer the conversation to a place I don't want to go yet. "Pregnancy. Motherhood."

I shrug. I knew he'd bring it up, but I don't want to talk about it, not yet, because what can I say? I hiss, "Lower your voice. My bodyguard is right outside."

He rolls his eyes. "Ror. You still haven't told them yet, have you?"

"No...it's not really an over-the-phone conversation. I want to tell them in person."

"Have you thought about *what* you're going to say?"

"I thought I'd just put a bow on my stomach and plant myself under the Christmas tree."

"Seems legit. Don't forget the gift tag. *To: Whose Sperm It May Concern.*"

I laugh. I have to laugh. If I don't laugh, I'll panic. I've been half-panicking since I missed my period over a week ago. Oscar is the only one who knows I'm pregnant right now...and that's only because I held him hostage on the phone while waiting for the test results to show up on the little stick all while ranting *we use protection* and *except for that one time* and *but why now, right now?*

My stomach has been in knots since, and it's more than morning sickness. I haven't got the *slightest* idea how to break the news to Ben and Roland...or how they're going to take it.

If tonight proved anything to me, it's that the world is barely ready for a polyamorous prince, let alone one with a *baby* attached. So I've extended my Berlin trip, made up excuses for my delay in Germany, and procrastinated, procrastinated, procrastinated.

"Oscar…" I start, and I know he can hear the worried whine in my voice because he cuts me off.

"They love you," he says. "No matter what. You'll figure this out."

I know he's right…but that doesn't quell the jitters.

I can hear the doorbell ring in the background. Oscar glances toward it once, his mouth pulled into a frown. "That's Francesca."

Oscar looks pained, and I know he would call off the office party just to spend the night calming me down. But I'm not about to let him do that. For the first time, Oscar is able to go on his own adventures, and there's no way I'm letting him hold himself back for me. "Go," I tell him. "Have fun. I'll be okay."

"Are you sure?"

"I promise. No way I'm letting you get out of public sweater humiliation."

He grins. "You're a freak, Ror."

"Takes one to know one. Love you, Otter."

"Love you, too."

With that, he ends the video message. Now that the room is silent, my anxiety starts sinking into my bones again. My heart pounds in my chest, and my head swims. I curl my fingers around the sink and stare at myself in the mirror. I don't look so much like a badass princess anymore. My fuzzy red hair poofs out, the remains of my makeup make my eyes look sleepless, and my T-shirt swallows me whole. It's one of Roland's, a Manchester United shirt, and I bunch it up to my face and inhale the smell of home—tea leaves, mint, and sandalwood. It makes my heart ache.

We've been through so much together…but what if this breaks the camel's back? It's a fear so real it knots in my throat.

Out of the corner of my eye, I see the pregnancy test sticking up like a flagpole in the bathroom trash bin. A spike of fear hits my heart—what if Sam sees it? Or housekeeping? I shove it down to the bottom and pile up tissues on top for good measure.

What've you gotten yourself into, Rory?

2

BEN

*S*omething is wrong.

There is no transition from *asleep* to *awake*; I open my eyes and I'm immediately on high alert. I check my senses. The bedroom is quiet, save for Roland's deep breaths beside me. His bare skin is hot against mine, and when I sit up, dried sweat makes the sheet cling briefly to my back. We're alone, but I can't shake the spine-tickling sensation of being watched.

My pistol sleeps in its holster on the bedside table. Roland doesn't budge, not even when I kiss the top of his head, pull the blankets over his shoulders, and slip out of bed. My clothes are on the floor (we made a mess of them last night), and it takes me a second to pick mine from his and redress in the dark. I slip my holster over my shoulders and exit the bedroom, closing the door as softly as I can on my way out.

The hallways of Helmsway Palace are bright, and I squint as my eyes readjust. The palace never sleeps. Two guards stand outside the prince's room—Thom and Lincoln—and I haven't checked the time, but if Thom is still here, it must be four or five in the morning. I nod to them and ask, "How's it?"

To which Thom responds, "All clear, boss."

Doesn't quell the discomfort rushing through my blood, however.

I know I must be a sight—hair askew, jaw unshaven—but the only person who could fire me for my unprofessionalism is *me*, and I decide to let myself off the hook this time. I walk barefoot down the hall and follow a familiar path through the kitchen (smells of tomorrow morning's scones and biscuits already baking), through the door disguised as a walk-in freezer, and down a staircase that leads into the basement security.

Back when I was Prince Roland's personal bodyguard, I used to practically live in here. So much so that he called it "my lair." Now that our relationship is less professional, more personal, I've been promoted to head of security, where I can keep an eye on the palace without actually being on the front lines anymore.

Which means I have less and less reason to be down here. I have my own office upstairs, complete with a view of the palace gardens. Still, I find myself returning to my lair on nights like this, when the whispers won't quit.

The lair is a small, closet-sized space, filled with television screens that show a live feed of every possible angle in Helmsway Palace. It's also not empty. My replacement sits in the swivel chair, eyes on the screen, large cup of coffee in front of him. He's a twenty-six-year-old pup whose name—much to Roland's amusement—is also Benjamin. But our name and loyalty to queen and country are all we share; we couldn't be more unalike.

"Boss!" Benjamin unfurls his legs from the desk and beams at me. "Top of the morning to you!"

"Benjamin," I mumble. *Hate*, Rory reminds me constantly, *is a strong word.* "How is it looking?"

"Just the usual, sir. There were a couple of stray cats that got into it on the South Lawn—a real doozy of a fight. You want me to play the tape back for you? Kept me on edge the whole time—I think everyone's all right, though."

"Any word from Rory?"

"Miss March got on her flight and is on schedule to touch down at 06:15. Do you think they serve pretzels on the plane? I was thinking the other day—why do they hand out peanuts? Allergies are so rampant these days, you never know what will set someone off."

My back molars grind. He's like a too-curious child tugging at my trousers, and it's far too early for this. "Go relieve Thom," I tell him. "I'll watch the monitors for a bit. Report back when Rory's touched down."

"Easy, peasy, lemon-no-problem, boss," Benjamin says in a voice so cheery, I want to easy, peasy squeeze lemon juice in his eyes.

He's lanky and has to bend his tall frame to exit the room. Finally, I'm alone. I take my old seat in front of the monitors. I'm taller than most, but no one is taller than Benjamin, and I have to adjust the seat so it fits me again.

The television monitors glow. This room hums. Didn't notice that until I started spending time away from it—it was all white noise before. But I hear it now. It drowns out the crackle in my brain. I slowly examine each monitor, letting my eyes prove to my nerves what I logically already know—everything is in its right place.

Benjamin left his mug. It says "Keep Calm And Hodor," whatever that means. It's leaving a coffee-colored ring on the desk, so I grab a tissue and wipe it down. While doing that, I notice the dust behind the monitor. The cleaning staff doesn't come in here; they don't have the clearance. I used to clean it, because unlike some *Bens*, I take fucking pride in my workplace. I pluck a couple more napkins out of the box and start wiping behind the monitors.

I see him coming on the screens, so I'm not surprised when the door clicks open. Nor do I turn around; I'm too busy hunting a dust bunny.

"How did I know I'd find you here?" Roland asks. I can hear the smirk on his lips.

"Just doing a little spring cleaning," I mutter.

"It's December."

"I'm getting an early start."

I'm bent on the desk to reach behind monitor four, and I nearly jump when he slips his hand up my backside and snakes it underneath my shirt. "We ought to get you a uniform to clean in," Roland says. "French maid, I'm thinking."

The noise that leaves me is a sigh—half-exasperated, half-distracted by the tickle of his fingertips on my bare skin, and not at all amused by his interruption. I pull away from under the monitors, drop the dusty tissue in the bin, and twist around to face him. There's not a lot of room in here—it's barely closet-sized—and Roland certainly isn't giving me any space, so I find myself wedged between him and my desk.

No—not *my* desk anymore. Benjamin's now. I frown at Roland. "You should go back to bed."

"My thoughts exactly," he says. "But only if you come back with me."

The offer is, admittedly, tempting. I love him like this; he hasn't made himself up for the public just yet. He's not the prince of England right now—he's just Roland. His blond locks are standing up in all directions like an electrocuted cat, his eyes are bleary, and he's wearing jeans and an open button-up that hangs uselessly around his shoulders, baring his svelte form. He looks unbearably handsome like this, and I wouldn't mind kissing the daylight out of him and lying down beside him.

But something pulls me back, anchoring me here. "I can't."

His eyebrows furrow. "You have work to do?"

"Something like that." The real answer—that I can't sleep, that the well of anxiety is rising in me and I can't stop it—stays glued to the roof of my mouth.

His frown softens. He leans in now so that our lips are almost touching. "Well," he murmurs thoughtfully, "if I can't move the mountain…"

His hands slip up my thighs, closing in on my groin. I'm practically sitting on the desk now, and my arms lock at my sides, fingers tightening around the edge of the desk.

"*Roland*," I plead. I want him to go. I want him to leave me to my demons and my lair.

But my protests are only half-hearted…and my prick is already half-hard. We both know that my declaration of his name isn't a *no*, and my meager dissent falls away as his lips find my throat. He kisses—purposeful, insistent kisses—all the way down my neck. When I feel his teeth graze my skin, I can't help the shudder that ripples through me.

I can't deny him. I can never deny him. I spoil him, I know that—what Prince Roland wants, Prince Roland gets. But he's my weakness—always has been—and all it takes is a couple of kisses and his hand cupping my crotch over my trousers and my resolve melts like butter.

There was a day when I'd only dream of us here. Before Rory pushed me to admit my feelings for Roland, I kept them caged inside. For six long, painful years, I was nothing more than his bodyguard and, at times, his trusted friend. His *mate* (that loathsome bloody word). And when the pressure got to be too much, when I needed an outlet for the frustration mounting inside of me, I'd come to this very room. I'd watch him on the monitors, feeling like a bloody pervert, hating myself, hating that I couldn't shake these feelings. All the while, I'd play out fantasies in my head.

Even my filthiest fantasies, however, had nothing on the real Roland. I could've never imagined how he could be—all with one kiss—playful and dominating, loving and teasing, boyish and arrogant and *mine*. He knocks the breath out of me with every kiss until, finally, he lowers himself to his knees and unzips my trousers.

His hands are soft, his touch so unlike my own—where mine are rough and calloused, his palms are warm and smooth. He wraps his fingers around my prick and I feel the blood rush, swelling to my full length at his touch. I know it delights him how quickly my body responds to his touch—he's like Tinkerbell, he needs applause to live—and those violet eyes of his practically sparkle when they meet mine. "Is this what you want?"

"Yes." My voice is so husky, so thick with lust already. I'm mesmerized as he begins to stroke me, slowly at first, taking his time working me up. Then his lips come into play, wrapping around the swollen, needy head. His tongue swirls, tasting the salt of me, and a groan rumbles deep in my throat.

"Quiet," he murmurs, his breath beating against my prick as his fist pumps my shaft, "don't want anyone bursting in here, do we?"

The prince loves a challenge—these are the little games we play, pushing one another's limits. And I must be a sucker, because I trap my bottom lip between my teeth so hard that I taste blood.

Roland licks me, pumping the parts of me he can't fit in his mouth, and I white-knuckle the edge of the desk as I struggle hard to keep my hips in place, even as everything is screaming in me just to grab his thick, blond hair and rut against his chin. But I let him set the pace, drawing me out, and it doesn't take long before he has me right where he wants me—sucking in tight breaths of air, pulse pounding, muscles taut on the brink of release.

I'm about to explode down the prince's throat when I hear the last voice I want to hear crackle on the radio. "Er, boss?" Benjamin says, his voice coming from the small hand-held on the desk. "Are you monitoring this line?"

"Fuck," I bark. Roland's lips pop off and leave me throbbing. "Don't answer it," I warn.

Too late—he stands and his deft hands grab the handheld radio before I can. "Copy that," Roland says, overpronouncing his vowels in the worst Cockney accent I've ever heard.

"I don't sound like bloody Oliver Twist."

He winks at me. Meanwhile, on the radio, Benjamin says, "Miss March's plane has just landed. She's on her way now."

"Jolly good, Benjamin. Over and out." Roland sets the radio aside and comes between my legs again. His palm slides up my tortured organ.

"You're a prat," I growl.

"So…you *don't* want me to finish you?" His fingertips ghost across my cock, keeping me on the painful edge. He nuzzles me; his warm breath hits my face, his lips trace my jaw, and he purrs, "Say it."

"Say *what?*"

"*Please, sir, I want some more.*"

I'm annoyed, pent up, and I want to *cum*, I don't want to laugh, but he's being such an impossible arse right now that I can't help the chuckle that leaves my throat. "You fuck—"

Suddenly, his fingers curl around my erection and his thumb circles the slickened tip of my prick, and the jolt of pleasure pulls a sharp gasp from me. I'll do anything, *say* anything to feel his lips, so I choke out, "Please, sir—"

That's all he needs before he's on his knees again, swallowing me whole. The moan I make is barely human, and my toes curl on the cold floor as I shoot down his throat. Roland lets out a soft, approving noise as he sucks my sanity from me, swallowing thick spurts of me until I don't have anything left to give. He cleans me with his tongue, making me shudder with the fucking bliss of it all, and finally releases me from his mouth, then tucks me back into my pants.

"Feel better?" he murmurs. He's kissing me sweetly now—my throat, under my ear—as I catch my breath.

"Mm." I can't form words. I've cum too hard to be a functional human for the next thirty to sixty seconds.

"Good." His lips press against mine now, gentle and loving and tasting like me. "Because you have to get dressed, and I have to brush my teeth. We can't keep our princess waiting."

3

ROLAND

*T*hree weeks. That's how long it's been since Ben and I have seen our pet. Our princess. Our Rory.

I'm not a patient man—I can admit that—and the hour it takes her to get from the airport to the palace is the longest, most excruciating hour of my life. I play a bit of piano, read half a chapter of Dorian Gray, and go through a couple games of solitaire. Ben is like a statue, unmoving, except every now and then he'll sigh and tell me to calm down—which I absolutely cannot.

Rory's home! I'm like a dog at the window, tail wagging in anticipation, whimpering for her to get here sooner.

My prayers are answered when the door opens. Rory comes strolling in, her rolling luggage in hand, bodyguard at her side. Immediately, my heart is in my throat.

She's a sight for sore eyes. Her ginger curls spill all wild out from under a black beanie. Her gaze finds us and she lights up in a smile. My girl loses all decorum in her excitement; she squeaks and comes running at us. I open my arms and she jumps into them. "My *God*, I've missed you!" she says.

"You're a bloody gift," I murmur in her ear. She laughs as I lift her up off the ground and cover her sweet, heart-shaped face with kisses. I want to be greedy with her, but I let her squirm out of my arms so she can skip over to Ben.

She tosses her arms around his shoulders, and he hugs her tightly. "Welcome home, kitten," he tells her.

The love in her eyes when she looks at him…it makes my heart swell. They kiss sweetly, deepening it only a moment before she pulls back just enough to tilt her head against his. A large smile cracks on her lips. "Mm. I love home."

"Wasn't the same without you," I tell her. It's true. I love Ben to the end of the earth and back—but nothing feels quite as right as it does when it's the three of us, like this. *Together.*

"You two been getting into trouble without me?" Rory asks, arching her eyebrows at the both of us.

Bashful Ben pulls his shoulders up in a tight shrug. "No more than usual."

I clasp my hand over Rory's shoulder. "Sit. Have some tea. Tell us all about your adventures."

She sits in the red armchair and slips out of her emerald peacoat to reveal a matching dress underneath. It brings out the green in her eyes, and I want to take her clothes off with my teeth. "I don't even know where to *start*," she exclaims. Ben and I sit on the armoire across from her, and a house-maid comes around with a pot of tea and an assortment of biscuits.

"How about with the Advent Day parties that kept you from us?" I tease. A little well-earned ribbing—Rory was supposed to come home nearly a week ago, but it seemed every day was some new German Christmastime tradition that she couldn't bear to miss.

"I *know.*" She makes a face. "Sorry. I'll tell you everything."

"Is everything all right?" We're all thinking it, but Ben's the one who asks the question point-blank. There's something *off* about Rory. She's always been excitable, but she's almost too jittery, fluttering around, an edge of franticness in every gesture.

"I'm fine," she says. She slips her hand over his and squeezes. "Really. I'm just tired. And in need of a shower and a nap."

"Well, you have about four hours for both before we go to Ben's parents'—"

Ben is shaking his head before I even finish. "We don't have to go right away," he comes out with quickly, as though the words were just waiting for any excuse to leap off his tongue. "Maggie will be there with the kids, and my parents will be occupied…"

"No, we *have* to," Rory confirms stubbornly, taking both Ben's hands in hers now to refocus him. "The only reason I came back was so I can see them."

"The *only* reason?" I ask, and she rolls her eyes.

"It's tradition," Rory explains. "Family is important. I wouldn't miss it for the world."

Ben hums a light noise, but his jaw is tightly set. Every year, he's spent Christmas Eve with his parents. I only know this because this year, for the first time, he invited Rory and me with him. To meet the family. I know he's looking for any excuse to get out of it—not because he's ashamed of us, or them, but because Ben is just not very good about talking about things like *emotions* and *love* and he's going to be fielding questions all night about the boyfriend *and* girlfriend he brought home for Christmas.

Truthfully, he's not the only one who's nervous. I've done charity work, and I've had PR shoots with Normal families, sure—nonroyal families, that is. But I've never actually sat down and had a *family dinner* with anyone who wasn't at least some duke's son. I haven't the faintest idea how one is supposed to act Normal.

For once, Rory and Ben are going to be entirely in their element and I'm going to be entirely out of mine.

"Are you sure?" Ben presses. "Because if you're not feeling well…"

"Ben Tolle, you're not squirming out of this one." Rory smiles. "Come on now, boys. Christmas waits for no one."

4

RORY

I don't get the chance to unpack—but that's on me. I've been so nervous about telling Ben and Roland about the pregnancy that I put off coming back to the UK until the very last second. And now I don't have time to unwind, slow down, and maybe have that single, very important conversation with my two boys. Instead, I barely have time to shower, get dressed, and reapply just a little makeup before Sam knocks on my bedroom door with a ten-minute warning, and then again with only five minutes to spare.

The third time she knocks, she doesn't stop hitting her knuckles against the door even after I shout that *I'm coming.* I throw the door open and instead of my five-foot compadre, find six feet of blond-haired, blue-eyed prince. Roland is wearing a nice, crisp suit and a half-cocked smile, and my annoyed frown flips itself.

"Hi, kitten," he says and invites himself in. It's immediately clear that this is not a friendly visit—it's *more than.* He closes the door behind me, scoops my face in his hands, and kisses me fully on the mouth. I whimper into his lips, and my body melts against his. Even though the thick, satin fabric of his navy suit I can feel his toned chest, his rippling muscles, and the exquisite length of his need for me.

His tongue swipes inside my mouth, all fire and want, and I clutch his shirt. I crave this, how *easy* our relationship is— no thinking required. Just pure love, unconditional acceptance, and raw, filthy passion. I'm lost in it, and for a moment, I forget about my secret, I forget about the buzz of people who hate what we are, I forget about all the negatives, and I remember that *this* is worth it, these men love me, and nothing else matters.

"Next time you take a trip," he murmurs breathlessly when we finally break apart, "leave your lips. I can't go so long without kissing them again."

"Only my lips?" I grin. "You don't want *any* other part of me?"

"Mmm," he hums, and his lips meet my jaw, then around the shell of my ear. "And your beautiful eyes. Your soft hair —" His fingers sift through my hair and then fall down my spine before cupping my rear. "—this lovely arse."

"And they say romance is dead," I chuckle.

"And let's not forget…the sweetest cunt I've ever tasted." As he growls those dirty words in my ear, his hand slips up my dress and between my legs. I gasp, my thighs tightening around his wrist as he cups me, rubbing my sex through my panties. I'm so wet already, *aching* for him, and his touch sends flames through my blood. My head falls against his shoulder, and I cling to him tighter, loving his hand and craving *more*—I want him to slip his fingers underneath the fabric of my panties and feel my slick, swollen slit.

It takes everything within me to grab his wrist and squeeze, stalling him. "Wait…wait," I breathe, my heart rabbit-thumping against my rib cage. "Christmas Eve. Ben's parents. Remember? We don't want to be late."

"I think the prince of England has earned the right to be a little late, don't you?"

There's something in his voice that makes me pause and look him in the eyes. "Are you nervous?"

His eyebrows lift. "Are *you*?" He traces a finger up the crease of my sex and it sends a full-body shudder through me. No way I'm going to focus like this, so I push his hand away, then take his face in both my hands.

"Focus," I tell him. "Roland. Are you scared to meet Ben's parents?"

He looks like an animal caught in a bear trap—as though he wants to squirm and joke his way out of it—but then he deflates, just a little, his shoulders dropping. "I've never met my boyfriend's parents before," he confesses. "Or my girl-friend's, for that matter."

"You have met my parents. On Skype. And they *love* you."

"That doesn't count."

The concern in Roland's eyes is genuine. For all his cocki-ness and boyish arrogance…I know there's a deep well of insecurity inside of him. His father was assassinated when he was only a boy, and Roland's paranoid queen mother closed him up inside the palace after that. She wouldn't let him leave, nor would she let anyone in. For ten years, the only people he interacted with on a daily basis were his mother, the staff, and Ben, his bodyguard. The experience left his social skills a little stunted; large crowds exhaust him, a single outing sends him into a twenty-four-hour recovery period in the palace library, and every now and then he'll pronounce a word strange because he knows how it looks on paper but not how it sounds on his tongue in casual conversation.

We're opposites in that way—he's an entertainer and can effortlessly command a crowd when all eyes are on him, but privately Roland is an introvert, who prefers the quiet. Me, I thrive off the energy from other people, but as soon as I'm in front of a crowd, I get shy.

Which is, maybe, half the reason we make such a good

team. I slip my hands down his arms to sooth him. "They'll love you," I tell him and mean it. "I promise. You're charming, you look amazing, and, most importantly, you love Ben. That's all parents care about. Let them see that and you'll win them over in no time."

Slowly, Roland's smile starts to return, his sky-blue eyes warming. "What would I do without you, kitten?" he asks and playfully cups my ear, scratching behind it.

I let out a small *mew* noise and lean into his touch. This is our game we play. He's my prince, I'm his kitten, and I feel safe—so safe—owned by him. I tilt my chin up, pliant, and he presses a soft, sweet kiss to my lips.

"Miss March, your car—oh." Sam stops herself short in the doorway and coughs once into her fist. "My apologies, Your Highness. Didn't see you there."

"No apologies necessary, Sam," Roland says. When he pulls back from me, the worry has left him and his old, familiar mischievousness flickers in those now-violet eyes. "We're coming."

I wish I was cumming, I think to myself, but I swallow the thought down, straighten my dress back over my thighs, and follow Roland out the door.

* * *

BEN'S FAMILY used to live in a run-down neighborhood on the South Side—his words, not mine—but since he started working for the royal family, he bought them a town house in Bristol. It's not far—about a two-hour drive—but my travels have taken it out of me, and I snuggle between my boys and promptly fall asleep on Roland's shoulder. I slip in and out of consciousness, catching flashes of England through the tinted windows—the emerald green beauty of the Hammersmith Bridge, the great twin peaks of the Bristol Cathedral, the spires of St. Nicholas, and, finally, the old city houses that look medieval, with sand-colored stone walls, intricate gargoyles, and cobbled streets.

We're outside of the city now in a quieter, suburban neighborhood when the car comes to a full stop and Ben gently nudges me awake. I completely come to my sense when I step out of the car and cold air whaps me in the face. It's a refreshing chill, though, not as snow-deep, bone-cold as Germany was, and I welcome it.

Roland is wearing a brown leather jacket with gray fur lining and suede gloves, while Ben's long figure is wrapped up in a slim, dark peacoat. They're both carrying gift bags while I've got one of the larger presents in my arms, and I fall in step between them as we walk down the cobblestones.

"His name is Ernest," Ben says. "My mother is Marie. Maddie is my sister, and the kids are—"

"Poppy and Charlotte," Roland interrupts smoothly. "Five and seven. Poppy plays piano, and Charlotte fancies herself a ballerina."

Even the golden amber of the dying sun doesn't hide the twitch of a near smile that forms on Ben's mouth. "Exactly."

His parents' town house is almost indistinguishable from the other townhomes on the block, except each is painted its own unique, bright color. Theirs is robin-egg blue. Our bodyguards, Sam and Benjamin, leave us here and wait in the car. We scale the steps, and Ben knocks on the door. Roland stares at the unopened door like he's about to go head-to-head with Medusa, so I slip my hand in his gloved one and give it an encouraging squeeze.

When the door opens, an older, portly man about as tall as I am stands in front of us. He's wearing at least two sweaters and a tweed cap over his receding hairline. When he sees us, his eyes crinkle and a smile stretches across his face.

"Yer Highness." He drops his head briefly. "Ain't e'ryday we get royalty in here, eh?"

"Roland, please. Call me Roland." Roland sticks his hand out. "Happy Christmas."

"Oi, Marie!" Ben's father calls over his shoulder. "I'm shaking the bloody prince's hand!"

"Let them in out of the cold, won't you, Ernest?" Marie swiftly comes over, pushing her husband out of the way to let us in. Ben gets most of his looks from her, I think; they both look like crows masquerading as humans—imposingly tall and lanky with jet-black hair. But he's got his father's eyes—a gentleness in them—and it warms me to see them in Ernest's face. Marie takes her son in her arms (*good to see you, Ben*) before addressing Roland and me with slightly more restrained enthusiasm than her husband.

Personally, I like Ernest's jolly, brazen attitude, and he puts a hand on my shoulder, squeezes, and says warmly, "Take a butchers at this beauty."

"Don't you over-egg the pudding, Ernest," Marie hisses.

I thought I'd heard it all after living in England for nearly two years, but suddenly I'm as lost as I was in Germany. Not only are they using phrases I've never heard before, but both of them—especially Ernest—has this thick, overextended accent that swallows up all the important parts of the word. "It's a pleasure to meet you!" I chirp. "Merry Christmas!"

"Happy Christmas to you as well," Marie says.

Ben takes control of the situation and hands over the gift bags. "We brought wine. And gifts."

We squeeze out of the narrow hallway and enter into a cozy living room where Marie points to the Christmas tree in the corner and tells us to drop the gifts there. I set the presents down in their own corner and use the opportunity to really take in the house. It's cute. Really cute. I remember Ben saying that he grew up on the docks, and they've definitely carried a nautical theme through their new home—there's a steering wheel hanging over the fireplace, decorative oars, and I even spot a little tugboat ornament on the tree. There are books everywhere, a newspaper strewn out over the table, and family photos hung on the walls.

There's a one of a little raven-haired boy with ripped jeans and a dirty shirt, glowering at the camera as he guts a fish that is half as big as he is. An older girl with his same bushy eyebrows has the fish head in her hand, and she's squishing its dead cheek against hers, matching the fish's open-mouth surprise. I can't help but grin. Humble beginnings, some might call it—but I just call it *family*. You can get through anything with people who love you.

"Oi! Mum, what'd I tell you about letting in the riffraff." I recognize the little girl in the picture almost immediately—Maddie, Ben's sister—even though she's gotten taller, older, and filled out around her middle. She has the same trouble-making grin as the girl in the photo, and she greets her younger brother by cuffing his ear. "Where the bloody hell you been, ay?"

"Maddie." Ben's voice is a low warning. "Do you recognize the company?"

"Excuse the piss out of me." She dips herself in a dramatic curtsy in front of Roland. "It's an honor, Your Highness."

But Roland's eyes only dance with amusement, and he matches her curtsy for curtsy. "The honor is mine, trust me."

"Rory." Ben gestures me over and I leave my place from under the tree to stand by his side. His hand falls to the small of my back. "This is our girlfriend."

Their girlfriend. I'll honestly never get tired of hearing that.

"Rory March, I know you." Her dark eyes sweep over me, assessing, and she cocks her head. "How the hell do you put up with these prats?"

"It's a labor of love." I spot a couple of pairs of eyes peeking around from the hallway. "Are those your girls?"

Maddie looks over her shoulder. "Cheeky monkeys! Come out!"

They're dressed in matching princess dresses, and they reluctantly peel themselves from around the corner. Eyes down, they pop into little unbalanced curtsies and mumble tiny-voiced greetings. Ben's nieces are so sweet, and my heart swells in my chest.

Roland squats down to be on their level. "All right…you must be Poppy and Charlotte."

The girls exchange looks of surprise and then nod.

"Well, think Santa got his addresses all mixed up, because he sent these to the palace…and I'm pretty sure they belong to you." He takes out two Toblerone bars, one with Poppy's name on it, the other with Charlotte's name.

The girls squeak with thanks, snatch up the chocolates, and go scampering off in their ballerina flats.

"Well, there goes their appetite for dinner," Maddie sighs, though I can tell she's quietly thrilled. "Who else is hungry, then?"

5

BEN

*D*inner goes better than expected. I tame my family best I can, but they've always been a rough bunch, and Roland and Rory seem entertained by it. I translate my father's thick accent to Rory at my side, my sister tempers her vulgarity, and, best of all, no one points at us and asks, *So, how does that work?*

The lot of them get along. It's strange to see both of my families together. Good strange. They fall in love with Rory immediately; her excitement is contagious. Roland quickly shakes off the *His Highness* remarks, and it doesn't take long before the dinner table has normalized.

After dinner, I excuse myself and slip outside. The sun has set, but Bristol is still lit up with strings of Christmas lights. The Avon River runs parallel to my parents' flat, and I can see the red and green anchor lights of a barge down the river. As my eyes follow the flow of black water, I catch a figure down the street. He's far away, sitting on a public bench, swallowed up in a large coat and a hat. He's got a camera in his lap, but he lifts it and snaps a couple of pictures my way.

My jaw clenches. I step off the porch and down the street.

The street is packed with cars, everyone home for the weekend, I suppose, except for the occupants in the black car at the end. I knock on the driver's side and the tinted window rolls down.

Sam greets me with a "Sir."

The smell of Mum's cooking wafts out of the car. Benjamin's sitting on the passenger side, and he lifts his party plate. "Miss March made us plates!"

Of course she did. Sneaky girl.

"How's everything?"

"All quiet out here," Sam says.

"What about him?" I tilt my chin to the cameraman on the bench.

"A particularly sticky reporter," Benjamin says between mouthfuls of Mum's chicken.

"Pain in the arse, more like it," Sam grumbles. "His name is Gideon Calder. Runs with *The Daily Gab*. We got his papers." She pulls up her phone and shows me a picture of his credentials.

Paparazzi, unfortunately, are just a fact of life now. There's not a lot more we can do besides tag them and keep an eye on them. Doesn't mean I have to like the fact that there's a man on my parents' street, monitoring their every activity.

Everyone else has gone home for the holidays. Why not this bloke?

"Keep an eye on him," I tell them.

"Will do, boss," Sam says.

"We've got this!" Benjamin echoes and sticks his thumb up.

He's not wrong. I'm micromanaging something that's already been managed. I hired Benjamin and Sam because they were the most qualified people for the job. I know I need to let go of the steering wheel, but every instinct just tells me to grip tighter.

Or maybe I'm just steering my thoughts about for what I'm planned tonight. I have a very special, very specific Christmas present for Roland and Rory in the pocket of my jacket, and I intend to give it to them tonight, when we're alone. It's a good thing—I know that, I've planned it through for weeks now—but it's not helping my nerves.

I light up a smoke and burn through it for a minute, trying to uncoil the tension in my veins. When the cigarette is no more than a nub, I kill it under my shoe and step back inside.

It's warm in the home. I hear my nieces running around and screeching with little-girl joy as Rory and Roland chase them through the house. The table is cleared, and I can see my mum in the kitchen, washing the dishes one by one. I drop my jacket over the back of a chair, roll up my sleeves, and step in beside her.

She smiles when I join her but then crinkles her nose at the cigarette smell. "Oh, Ben," she sighs. "You're not still smoking, are you?"

I can't help it—there's a teenage boy in me that still gets defensive every time my mum lets out one of her disappointed huffs. I feel my shoulders square off, and I scrub the sponge over her dishes a little too hard. "What of it?"

Out of the corner of my eye, I can see the pinch of her lips. "I don't understand how you can like a thing like that, is all."

"No. You don't."

"I don't understand" has always been her go-to. She didn't understand when she found out I liked boys—and understood even less when I corrected and told her that I like boys *and* girls. She didn't understand when I refused to bring friends over to our crumbling, black-mold-infested shoebox of a flat. She didn't understand why I couldn't just *pick* between Rory and Roland, why I had to have both. Her latest complaint—which she murmured to me when we'd walked inside—was that she just didn't *understand* why I'd hide such a nice jawline under the unshaven scruff I'd let grow out.

What am I going to say to that—*sorry, Mum, but my girlfriend likes the way it scratches her bare thighs when I lick her?*

No. She doesn't have to understand. She just has to live with it.

"They're not going away anytime soon," I say, perhaps too gruffly. "Maybe not ever."

Might be wishful thinking on my part, but…isn't that what Christmas is all about?

She must sense that I've tensed up, because she softens her approach after that. "I like them," she says. "Rory and the prince."

"So do I."

And then we lapse into silence, letting the rush of sink water do the talking for us. I'm comfortable here—the click of dishes, the shared activity of a mundane task—but my mum can only stay quiet for so long.

"Are you happy?" she asks.

"Yes, Mum."

"You just…seem stressed, is all."

I extend my silence by slowly rinsing off a plate. I can never lie to my mother. Her ability to see through me is a pain most days, and truthfully half the reason I spent so much time out of the house as a kid. But today, I decide to give a little.

"It's not them," I say, keeping my eyes on the dishes. "I agreed to stop being Roland's bodyguard. It was too complicated. I was always working when we went out and…I couldn't turn it off."

"Well, that's good," she says, with hesitant cheerfulness.

"Mm." Suds wash off the plate, off my hands, and I stack it in the dryer. "I don't know. I feel useless without it."

"I know the feeling," she says. "When you and Maddie

flocked from the flat, I didn't know what I'd do. I didn't know *who* I was if I wasn't your mum."

"What'd you do?"

"I started mothering your father. Lord knows he needs it."

We both chuckle at that.

Her hand reaches over and squeezes my arm. "Ben," she says seriously. "All those qualities that made you a good bodyguard…they're still there, you know. You're loyal. Protective. A hard worker. You just have to refocus your energy into something else."

"You make it sound easy."

"It's not. But if anyone's up for the job, my son is."

I cast her a look. Words I want to say stick to the roof of my mouth. She grants me mercy and takes a plate from my hands to dry it. "I'll finish these up. Go make sure your sister hasn't caused irrevocable damage to the royal family, please."

RORY

*R*oland is a monster.

A growling, stomping, toe-eating monster that can't stop, won't stop.

He chases Ben's two nieces around the house, down the hallway, and up and down the stairs. From my spot on the love seat nursing a cup of tea with Maddie, we can tell where they are from the thump of feet, the peals of little girls' laughter, and the occasional anguished cry of a defeated monster.

"Do you think we should rescue him?" I ask Maddie.

She shakes her head. "He gave them the chocolate—this sugar high is entirely on him."

As if on cue, Roland steps into the entranceway of the living room. He's short of breath, his blond hair disheveled, and he's got unicorn stickers on his shirt and face. He's also thrown little Poppy over his shoulder and she dangles down, her long hair brushing the floor, a Cheshire cat grin stuck on her lips as the blood rushes to her head.

"Anyone see a little girl run this way?" Roland asks and lifts his free hand to imitate her size. "About yea high, pink dress, very delectable little toes?"

Behind him, I spot little Charlotte crouching on the staircase, her little fingers gripping the bars as though she were in a jail cell. "Behind you!" I point, not even trying to hide how into this game I am. "On the staircase!"

"Nooo!" Charlotte screeches when he spots her, and then she screams with laughter as he starts to chase her up the stairs.

"You've got two really cool girls," I tell Maddie. "You must be proud."

"Yeah." Maddie shrugs. "They're all right."

I can't help the laugh that bursts from me at that. "*All right?*"

"Don't get me wrong—I love the buggers," she says, motioning to them. "But they're work, you know?"

I set my tea down so I can focus on her. "What happened to their dad?"

She snorts. "Oh, he's a cunt. He was into it, you know, all excited and everything. We got diapers, even went to my bloody Lamaze classes with me. Then as soon as the girls popped out—that was it. He was a fart in the wind, that one. You know…they think it's going to be all fun and playtime. They don't think about the sacrifice."

This conversation is hitting too close to home. I feel my heart tighten and start to burn in my chest. I rub the back of my neck and try to shake off the feeling. "I bet."

"I had to give up *everything*," Maddie continues, completely ignorant to my growing discomfort. "I mean, forget about art school. Or weekends in Italy. Or even finishing a bloody full movie without someone pulling on your leg for something or another. I was willing to give that all up, but Robbie? He bolted. I swear, for a bit there, I thought Ben was going to hunt him down and kill him. Hell, maybe he did—haven't seen a child support check in *months*, the prick."

The more Maddie prattles on, the harder my heart

pounds in my chest. Her words begin to fade, and my imagination kicks in—my worst fears spawning to life. Ben works, constantly, and Roland only just left his mother's clutches, only just started exploring the world on his own. What if they're not ready to make the sacrifices parenthood requires and I become another Maddie—bitter, overworked, and alone?

Can they give up everything to be parents?

Can *I*?

I can't hear a word she's saying—my eardrums have tightened into a shrill, piercing sound. My heart aches, my chest burns, and I can't catch my breath. *I will not have a panic attack in front of Ben's family.* I won't. But try as I can to avoid it, I feel it overpowering me all the same. I grip the arm of the chair and dig my fingers in, trying desperately to feel something *solid* connecting me to reality.

A hand touches my shoulder. I expect Maddie, but when I snap my gaze up, Ben is standing in front of me, quiet concern stamped across his face. "Rory. Can I borrow you for a moment?"

I can't speak, but I nod and let out a small *uh-huh* noise. He takes my hand and I let him lead me as though I'm a newborn kitten, blind and wobbly on my limbs. He guides me out of the living room, down the hall, and into a bathroom under the staircase. It's tight in here, the walls blindingly white, and my vision pulses with each struggling beat of my heart. There's tile on the floor, and I want nothing more than to strip out of this dress and lie on it, feel the cold against my back.

Ben closes the door and stands in front of me. His eyes search mine. "Are you having a panic attack?" he asks calmly.

"Yes," I rasp.

"Do you want me to...?"

"*Please.*"

He doesn't need me to tell him twice. Ben's hand slips

around my throat, holding me. And then, slowly, he tightens his grip. My back rests on the bathroom door. I move my hand to his wrist—but not to stop him. To pull him closer. I feel him adjust—his hands are huge, fingers long, calloused, and I feel him move so his grip is directly underneath my jaw. Then his thumb and forefinger squeeze together on the side of my neck. Everything in me focuses on the pressure of his hand. My breath gets light, my eyelids flutter closed, and my head spins. All I can feel is *Ben*, my Ben, and suddenly nothing else matters: I'm safe in his arms, safe here, safe, *safe*. I relish this feeling and relief washes over me, dampening my panic.

I've been having panic attacks my whole life. Ben is the only one who's ever been able to snap me out of them. The second his hand is around my throat, all my fear and anxiety trickles out of me, a low buzzing in my blood that tingles down to my fingertips and toes. We found the solution more or less by accident, and now it's the only thing that calms me down. I waver here, let the moment last, and slowly the rest of the world falls into focus again. I can hear Ben murmuring lowly in that calm, steely voice of his: *It's okay. You're okay.*

I've had enough—any more and I'll lose consciousness— so I tap the back of his hand with my forefinger twice. It's my signal, my safe word when we're like this. Immediately, he releases his grip, but he keeps his hands loose around my throat, just touching me now. I gasp and a rush of cool air crystalizes in my lungs.

The entire experience is soothing, freeing, and erotic; my body is humming, alive for him now. Ben kisses the corner of my eye, my cheek, and my ear. The scruff of his jaw scratches my face, and I cling to him.

"Thank you," I whisper.

He pulls back just enough to look at me. Now, I see the concern flickering in his dark eyes. "I thought you stopped having panic attacks."

I shrug weakly. "So did I. I guess it just…happens sometimes."

His expression softens. He tucks a small strand of my hair behind my ear. "How do you feel now?"

Warm. Aroused. Safe. Loved. "Better."

He tilts his forehead to mine and then presses a small, sweet kiss to my lips. I whimper and savor it, pressing in deeper, as though his kiss is the only thing keeping me pinned to this world. He allows it and extends the moment for a minute longer before he seals it off.

My secret feels so heavy now—a rock in my throat. I can't wait any longer. They'll either love me and this baby, or they'll leave us in the dust—and the pain of not knowing which is suddenly unbearable. "Can we…talk?" I ask. "Alone? Just the three of us."

Ben nods. "I'll tell them we're turning in."

"I'll be right out."

He takes my hand, curls it around his, and presses a kiss to the back of my fingers. With that, he leaves, closing the door softly behind him.

I'm alone now. I go to the bathroom mirror. My eyeshadow has smudged a little. Occasionally, when Ben chokes me, it opens up the waterworks, and I don't even realize I've been crying until I taste salt. I turn on the tap and wash my cheeks, fixing up my makeup.

Out of the corner of my eye, I notice there's a window in the bathroom. I could probably stand on the toilet lid and crawl out of it. Escape to New Zealand. Or Moscow. Or *anywhere.* Just run, far, and never come back.

But I can't. No matter where I went, my heart would still be here. In Helmsway Palace, with the two men I love more than life itself.

"You're Rory March," I tell my reflection in the mirror. "And you can do this."

7

BEN

*W*e say good night to my parents and Maddie. They wrap their arms around Rory and Roland, wish them Happy Christmas, and beg them to come back soon.

Roland has run Poppy and Charlotte ragged, and I can't bear to wake them up. I leave the two girls snuggled up on the couch and promise their mum we'll come by for breakfast, at least, before we're back on the road again.

We exit their flat, and I think the bite of the cold does Rory some good because I can already see the color returning to her cheeks.

"We're not spending the night with your family?" Roland asks as he pops his collar against the chill.

"Not quite." I have one more surprise left for them.

The River Avon shushes against the bank. We walk along it until we reach the floating dock. There's a small ladder to get to the dock, and I toss my leg over the edge to get to it. I step onto the dock and take Rory's hand, helping her down as the planks bob underneath our feet.

"Welcome to *The Red Lady*," I tell them. "The owner is an

old friend. Borrowed her for the night on the condition that we bring her back in one piece."

A boyish grin grows across Roland's face, and Rory gasps. "Oh my god...this is *so cool*."

The Red Lady is a crimson, sixty-foot cruiser narrow boat that stretches the length of the dock. She's thin as an arrow with holiday lights strung up along the side, giving her a festive look. Rory squeaks with delight and clambers aboard before I can even attempt to do the gentlemanly thing and give her a hand. Roland, meanwhile, clamps his hand over my shoulder and says, "Well done, mate."

I'm so fucking proud of myself, I don't even mind the *mate*.

It's a step up to get onto the deck, where the tiller has been raised up; we're not unmooring tonight. Rory bounces around until I fish out the key the unlocks the double doors to the cabin and let her in. As she and Roland head below deck, my eyes sweep the horizon—

And I see him. That bloody fucking cameraman is *still there*. Sitting on the bench like a shadow. Waiting. Watching.

I make a note to myself to pull all the curtains shut and follow them inside.

Rory's already darting about excitedly. It's about as slim as a train car, with curtained windows on either side. A couple of steps down and the cabin opens up to a galley with mirrored cushioned benches, a small kitchen, a WC, and bed in the stern. Heating is an issue since it's not very insulated, but as long as we're docked, we're plugged into the electricity. I've already got two space heaters going on either end of the boat, which makes it cozy enough as long as the doors are closed.

There's a bottle of champagne, too, chilling on the kitchen counter with three flutes beside it. Roland immediately goes to the champagne. "Happy Christmas!" he shouts as he pops off the cork. I wince, expecting it to break a window, but mercifully it bounces off the ceiling and hits the floor. Rory laughs as he fills up the glasses.

"No—thank you," she says, putting her palm out when he shoves the glass in her face.

"Not feeling celebratory?" Roland asks.

"No, it's…" Rory starts to pace in the small kitchen. "Um. Well. You two should drink. A lot. Ben—get started." She plucks up a glass and hands it over to me. "Actually, why don't you both just down those and I'll refill you."

She's frantic again. That same nervous flicker in her eyes that I saw in the flat before her panic attack. Slowly, as though approaching an easily startled deer, I set my glass on the table and try, "Why don't we sit down?"

I tug all the shades closed, so now the only lighting comes from the soft glow of the copper lamps tucked into each corner of the boat. Rory guides us so Roland and I are sitting side by side on the portside bench while Rory sits directly across from us. Roland—love the bloke, but he's slow to the pickup—grins as he glances between the two of us, takes a sip of champagne, and then says, "What's all this, then?"

"So…when I went to Germany. It was great. Lots of fun. And I wanted to come back sooner, it's just…then I found this thing out, and I wasn't sure how you guys would take it. I mean, I know you both love me, and I love *you*—but it's so easy to get in your head about these things, you know? And all the worst-case scenarios were spinning around and I just—"

"Rory." Roland's voice interrupts her. "Kitten…whatever it is, we're here for you."

"Okay." She smiles. Or tries to smile. She's panicking, it's clear as anything. I can read it in her face and in the way she rambles. She looks at the floor, rubs her hands over her thighs, and them mumbles to herself, "Rip the Band-Aid off, Rory."

She looks at us, exhales a deep breath, then says the two words that change everything:

"I'm pregnant."

8

_____

RORY

*I*t's hard to tell what either of them are thinking for a while. They both stare at me for what seems like a millennia, and I have to remind myself I've had two weeks to process this information. They've only had two seconds.

"You're pregnant?" Roland parrots my words, as though he misheard me.

I nod. "Pregnant. As in…with child. And it's one of yours—"

Suddenly, Roland stands and immediately swoops me up in his arms. I yelp in surprise as he spins me around the narrow boat. "You're pregnant!" he shouts again.

Not angry shouting. Not concerned. Happy. He's happy for me. Happy for us.

I laugh. *I laugh.* This is the first time since I've found out that I've allowed myself to feel any kind of joy about this. The burden of keeping this secret nearly killed me, but now that it's out, and now that they're responding with happiness, not anger, I feel a sense of relief flood through me. "Yes! I am!"

"Rory." Roland lets me back on my feet and grabs me by

either side of my face. "That's wonderful. I love it. And I love you."

"I love you, too…" I murmur before he plants a hard, passionate kiss on my mouth, then another, and another.

"So you're…happy?" I ask, still stunned that this is going over so easily.

"Happy?" Roland asks. "I'm over the moon."

Ben is standing as well. I turn to him and immediately grip his shoulders. "And you?"

"I'm happy, too," Ben reassures me. He isn't as outwardly celebratory as Roland, who is animated in his joy. Ben is reserved, but his eyes are glassy, and I can tell this news has had a profound effect on him, too.

"Are you sure?" I ask.

"Yes. This is…the best thing that could ever happen to us."

He presses a gentle kiss to my mouth and I'm so over-whelmed with relief, I want to cry. The next words come spilling out of me. "I just…I was so afraid when I found out. I knew I had to tell you, but there's so much—like, who will be called Daddy? Are we all going to live at the palace? Does this make my child part of the royal family—?"

Ben stops me by taking my hands and giving them a squeeze. "There's going to be…a lot of decisions that have to be made," he agrees. "But…that's going to take a while to sort out. For right now…let's just enjoy this moment."

It's not like Ben to live in the moment—Ben, who is always ten steps ahead of everyone else, constantly worrying about the next meteor to hit. So if he wants to savor this for a second…who am I to say no?

Fuck it. I'm pregnant, I have two loves in my life, and I deserve to be happy about that.

Before I know it, I'm clinging to Ben. My fingers clutch his shirt, my lips smother his, and I whimper against his mouth. He holds me close, cradling me, as his tongue slips past my lips and tastes me. Roland comes up behind me—I can feel him brush my hair to the side as he presses a kiss to the back of my neck, his lips marking the path down my spine.

I need my independence, I need my space, and I need the ability to do what I want when I want to do it. But…God, did I miss my men. I missed their lips on me, their hungry kisses, their loving touches and hard bodies. When Ben finally breaks away, we're already panting for breath and my body is humming.

"Should we…move this to the bed?" I venture hopefully.

"Yes," Roland murmurs heatedly in my ear. "Definitely."

There's a zipper down the back of my dress, and Roland peels it away, his lips connected with each bare patch of skin as it's exposed. I shimmy out of my dress, letting it puddle on the floor, and now I'm wearing nothing but my panties, a bra, and my heels. I used to hate heels—only combat boots for this girl. Boots are still my go-to, but for moments like this? When I'm mostly naked and balancing on spikes? I feel powerful—and hot. And the greedy touches and kisses of my two men only inflate my confidence.

Ben slips his arms around me and, before I know it, he's lifted me off my feet. I squeak and wrap my legs and arms around him, and he kisses me as he carries me down the narrow hallway and lays me onto the bed. There's not exactly a "bedroom" per se; it's more of a mattress on a raised shelf, with a round window in the wall. The curtain is pulled, but I can still see ripples of night-black water outside.

Ben unhooks my bra, tosses it, and kisses down my chest. My nipples are already raised into tiny pink nubs, and he presses a kiss to each of them before going south. He catches my heel in his hand and carefully undoes the strap, slowly, in a way that shouldn't be nearly as sexy as it is. Roland rips off his clothes, lets them fall to the ground, and then he's beside me, tilting my head so my lips meet his.

It's a big bed (thank God) and the three of us fit in it

snugly but comfortably. Ben sets my heels down, then draws my panties off my legs so I'm completely naked under them. Ben is the only one dressed now, and Roland and I both take turns stripping Ben of his suit and tie.

By time the three of us are all bare, my body is buzzing. For the most part, when I travel, I'm able to ignore how much I *miss* my men, but now that I'm back, I feel every day that I was gone. The ache compounds and I feel my nether lips swell until they're painfully puffy and wanting. But even then, I don't get what I want. Not right away. I'm trapped between these two hard-as-steel men who just want to worship me; they savor my body, and I savor theirs. For a long while, we just lie together, the three of us, naked, kissing, touching. Ben's body is hard, muscled, sharp as cut glass, while Roland is softer, warmer, a roaring hearth on a winter's night, his blond hair tickling me where Ben's beard scratches.

My pleasure and pain, wolf and lion, devour me and leave me dizzy. I feel hot breath on my neck, fingers through my hair, a warm touch on my hip, caressing my leg, and I lose track of what belongs to who. We tangle together, limbs wrapped around limbs. They're hot, and so am I, and every time fingers graze my skin or a pair of lips teases the sensitive bits around my breasts and my throat, I feel my ache grow stronger.

I don't know how long we stay like this, but it feels like hours spent diving into each other, and when my legs press together, I feel my wetness sticking down my thighs.

"I need you," I whisper to no one in particular—I just need *one* of them inside of me.

Roland is the closest to the edge of the bed, and he rolls over to grab his pants off the floor, riffling around in his pockets. "What are you doing?" I ask him.

"Getting a condom."

I stroke my fingers through his hair, waiting for him to

47

come to the realization on his own, and when he doesn't…I press a kiss under his ear and ask innocently, "Why?"

"So you don't…*oh.*" He chuckles, turns to me, and catches my chin between his fingers. "I suppose I don't have to worry about knocking you up, do I?"

I bite my lip and shake my head. "A little late for that."

His mouth tastes like bitter tea and peppermint. I get lost in it, as Ben kisses the back of my neck and coaxes my leg up around Roland's hip. Those fingers between my thighs— those are Ben's—I know because they're rough, calloused, and eager to feel me. He pets my sex, warming me, smearing my wetness across my hot folds, and I shudder. I feel my prince shift against me, reaching between us, and then Ben's fingers are replaced by Roland's stiff shaft. The bulbous head of him parts my nether lips and, even though I can't bear one more second without him inside of me, still he teases me here. He rubs it up and down my slit, and the friction is both deliriously lovely and agonizing. I whimper, digging my nails into his shoulder, parting my legs even farther, wantingly.

"Tell me what you want, kitten," Roland purrs.

"Please," I beg. "I want you inside of me."

He finally gives me what I need. Roland presses inside of me and I feel my body stretch to accept his girth. I'm so wet, he slides in easily, but still he does it slowly, forever careful not to hurt me. I throw my head back and gasp, my legs tightening around his hips, drawing him deeper. Roland moans my name, his face in my breasts, as Ben nips my neck and growls, his voice gravelly with lust, "Good kitten."

Ben's arm draws around me, his hand slips over my throat, adding pressure, and I feel so full and so safe I could cry. Roland's hips roll like the ebb and flow of the river outside, and I swoon, tracing my fingers down his side, clinging to him. Having him bare—completely bare—inside of me is a new treat, and I love the way his body nestles against mine. I want every inch of him so there's no empty space between us.

I want it to last forever, but eventually Ben moves his hand to the back of Roland's head to get the other man's attention. When Roland looks up, his eyes are burning, that violet fire alight in them.

"Take her in your lap," Ben says. So Roland does. He slips out of me, and I feel so empty that a whimper leaves me, a sound similar to the cry of a kitten. The two of them manipulate my pliant body so I'm just where they want me. The trust I have for them is unconditional. Roland sits up and turns me so I'm sitting in his lap now, with my back to his chest. He kisses the back of my neck and then eases inside of me once more. I sit back until he's in me to the hilt. I feel so full at this angle, and I brace myself on Roland's thighs.

I barely get to catch my breath before Ben steps off the edge of the bed. He catches a handful of my hair and kisses me. I sigh into his mouth, and his lips travel lower. They brush my breasts and he finds my nipple, teasing it with his tongue first before pulling it between his lips. Before I know it, his hand slips between my legs. His finger grazes my clit and I gasp, the friction sending a lightning bolt of pleasure through me. He traces circles around my exposed, sensitive nub, then pets my swollen nether lips wrapped around Roland's cock.

My fingers dive into Ben's short hair, and I moan loudly. I'm trapped between them, and there's nothing I can do but let my men lavish me with torrents of pleasure. Roland hugs my belly and thrusts upward into me, and each time he does, it's so deep and hits *that spot* inside of me. Ben is merciless, tugging my nipples between his teeth as he rubs me, slips a finger inside and rubs Roland *inside* of me, and the sensations make me start to quiver, my legs trembling.

"Oh God," I whimper, my voice breathy and weak. I drop my head back against Roland's shoulder and roll my hips, gripping Ben's hair, grinding against his touch. The words tumble from me, mindless pleas and moans: "Oh my God... please...just like that!"

I'm panting, my chest heaving with every breath, and I feel my body constrict around Roland and everything in me get tight and achy. Ben sucks my breast hard enough to leave a mark. All of my focus centers on the flick of Ben's finger at my swollen nub and the sensation of Roland's cock hitting just the right spot inside of me. Every part of me stimulated, I begin to whimper and tremble. The human body wasn't built to withstand this much pleasure all at once—I'm almost certain of it—because when I cum, it's a Category Five Orgasm. I shout and I grip them both—Ben between my legs, Roland behind me—as my back arches sharply. They don't let up: Ben flicks and rubs my sensitive skin as it throbs and pulses around Roland's thick organ, and Roland kisses my ear, my throat, and calls me a good girl, a good kitten, just like that, *that's my girl*—

I'm a shivering, whimpering, endorphin-delirious mess.

"Please," I beg, "no more."

Only then does Ben remove his hand from between my legs. He does cup my face, however, and draw me in for a heated kiss. I taste his need. His kisses are rough, Roland is still rock hard inside me; my boys' stamina is *insane*, and I need to catch my breath.

"Wait, wait, wait," I plead against Ben's mouth.

"What?"

"Please...just...one second." I'm all flailing limbs as I awkwardly climb off Roland and flop down on the bed. My whole body is humming, and I feel noodle-limp. "I just need to catch my breath."

"That's fair," Roland remarks, even though I know they're both still buzzing, both can still go, go, go all night, like the Terminators they are.

Roland's hair is totally wild right now from where I

grabbed at it, his normally coiffed lion's mane all bushy. Ben frowns at it and, with a single swift flick of his finger, pushes a clump of hair from Roland's eyes.

"Thanks, mate," Roland says.

"Don't mention it."

The little scene is so incredibly adorable…it gives me an idea. I grin and bite my lip. "Can I make a request?"

"Anything."

"Can you make love…to each other? Like you do when I'm not here?"

They exchange a look. They do that a lot—talk with their eyes. Even I don't always know what they're saying. "I think we can manage that," Roland responds.

"Bagsy," Ben says quickly.

To which Roland replies with a short laugh, "All right, then. Let's give our kitten a show."

He slips his hand through Roland's hair and captures his mouth in a heated kiss. The other man moans in his mouth as Ben climbs back into the bed, on top of Roland. I get comfortable and sit up, resting my back against the wall.

Ben is a lethal man; he can (and has) killed to protect me and Roland. But in bed? His hands are gentle, and he uses his body to pleasure us, not to hurt us—at least, not a *bad* hurt. I watch as he savors Roland's body, his lips grazing Roland's throat and his strong chest. The dim light casts angular shadows over the muscles on Ben's back as he dips his head to nip Roland's hip.

Jesus. They are the most beautiful men I've ever seen. And to see them both lost in each other…it's a major turn-on. My body starts buzzing again, throbbing, and I can't help it—my hand slips between my thighs. My clit is already so sensitive, and when I touch it and start to rub in slow circles, a bolt of pleasure rushes through me. I can't touch myself as well as Ben can touch me, but it helps alleviate the need.

"On your hands and knees, prince," Ben murmurs.

Roland obeys, shifting up, as Ben reaches over to grab his bag. He pulls out a small container of lube, which he coats his hand with before slipping a finger between Roland's cheeks. Ben's bicep flexes as he fingers the prince, warming him up. I know how good those hands feel inside me, and watching them work inside Roland makes me shudder. Roland lets out a low groan and mutters, "Fucking hell…whatever you're doing, don't stop."

Roland's toes curl and so do mine. I'm so slippery that it's hard to gain friction against my clit. Ben's attention focuses on me suddenly and I gasp and my hand freezes. I don't know why—obviously, we're all aroused here—but this is different, being a voyeur. I'm so wrapped up in watching *them* I've almost forgotten that they can see me, too.

But Ben only grins. "Come here, kitten."

Kitten. Just the word makes my throat tighten with need. I crawl closer and he nods toward Roland. "Kiss him."

I sidle up next to Roland. His deep blue eyes lock onto me, hazy with need, and when I press my lips to him and he kisses me back, he's sloppy, hungry.

"You want to stroke his prick?" Ben asks.

Immediately, my eyes travel down, where Roland is swollen and leaking. I want to do more than stroke him. I want to lick the salt from his tip, take him inside of me, and ride him until I cum so many times that I black out. But I know that's not the answer Ben is looking for. Instead, I bit my lip and nod. "Yes."

"Do it," Ben says. "Slowly."

I reach down and grasp Roland in my hand. He's iron hard, but his skin is so velvet smooth, and he moves easily through my fingers. I realize then that he's still slick from me, and that makes me ache so badly I grind a little against the mattress.

Roland is clearly enjoying it. I get lost in kissing him, the tangle of our tongues, and the way he feels in my grip. His hips move to meet my hand, jerking, losing rhythm, and then Ben chides, "I said *slowly*."

I didn't realize I'd sped up, but now Roland is panting, throbbing in my hand. *Whoops.* "Yes, sir, sorry," I blabber.

"Hands off each other," Ben says, so I pull my hand away reluctantly.

Suddenly, Roland's eyebrows knit and he drops his head, blond hair dripping down. He lets out a couple swears and reaches back to grip Ben's hip, which is now pressed tightly against his own. Ben's inside of him now, and he kisses Roland's shoulder blades.

"Is that okay?" Ben murmurs.

"More than," Roland gasps.

Ben's command to keep my hands off Roland is suddenly unbearable. He looks so good like this—soaked in his own lust and uninhibited—and I want to touch and kiss him all over. I sink my fingers into the mattress instead, balling up the fabric, and grind myself harder against it, looking for friction, any friction, just something to ease the ache burning between my legs.

"Do you want him inside of you, Rory?" Ben asks, and his words bring me back to earth.

I nod frantically. "Yes…more than anything."

Ben's hand reaches around and pumps Roland's cock, slowly, from base to tip and back again. He's teasing Roland —and teasing me with the sight of it. "Ask for it."

"Please," I beg. "Please…I want it inside of me… I want it so badly…"

"Get underneath him, then," Ben says.

I scramble to get under Roland, flat on the mattress. The second I do, Roland kisses me, swallowing my tongue in his mouth. I feel Ben guide Roland's cock against my slit, and then he pushes it inside of me. Roland and I both gasp at the same time, and I shift to take him in deeper, my thighs clutching his hips, clutching Ben's hips, too. The three of us are tangled together, both of my men on top of me, rolling as one wave. Roland's fingers grip my hair, and Ben's hand tightens around my thigh. I'm pinned under them—and there's no place I'd rather be. The combined body heat makes me sweat, my back clinging to the sheets, my skin sticking and unsticking to Roland's bare body.

It's hot, intense, but it's more than that—it's love, pure love, our bodies moving in the same rhythm, our hearts beating in sync. I'm breathing in Roland; Ben's electricity stirs in my blood. They are part of me, and I am part of them. Yes, I love sex for the pleasure it gives me—but I also love sex because it's the physical form of the one thing I can never seem to put into words: *I am inside you, you are inside of me.*

I want this to last forever, but I can feel the heat between us climbing. The flow of our bodies becomes less even as we twist, writhe together, and finally—it snaps.

I bury my face into Roland's shoulder and cry out, whimpering through an orgasm so powerful, it's almost painful. Roland fills me—the essence of him spilling over and in me. Ben moans. For a while, I see stars, and I try to catch my breath as my body thrums and throbs.

Roland's lips catch mine, and we kiss in a daze. And then my men share a hot, sweet kiss. I taste Ben's lips last, and I lick at the inside of his mouth, nibble his stubble.

"Stay here," Ben says. He gets up, so I climb closer to Roland. He's gone only a moment before he comes back with a towel. "Spread your legs, kitten," he tells me. I do, and the towel feels damp and warm when he rubs it gently over my sex and my cum-stained thighs.

"Thank you," I say.

Then he does the same to Roland, taking care of us like the spoiled brats we are, before he puts the towel away and snuggles up with us. Once again, I'm caught between them— my favorite place to nestle up.

"Let's never go that long without shagging again," Roland murmurs.

"Agreed," I purr, resting against Ben's chest. "That was…"

"Amazing," Ben fills in for me.

A comfortable silence stretches between us as each of us catch our breath.

"I have one question," I say after a moment.

"What's that?" Ben asks.

"What's *bagsy*?"

They laugh in unison. It's an amazing sound. No—it's my *favorite* sound.

"I think you have it in America," Roland says once he's stopped laughing. "But it's called something else. Dibbing?"

"Dibs?" I ask.

"Right. Like…claiming first rights to something."

"So *bagsy* is…"

"Top bunk," Ben states.

I roll my eyes. "Boys and their euphemisms."

"You don't know the half of it."

Ben's arm curls around me. His hand rests at my belly in a way that feels purposeful. All at once, I'm acutely aware again of the life growing inside of me. I lace my fingers in his, keeping it there.

The waves lap against the side of the boat. A foghorn goes off in the distance. I can hear Roland's heart pounding in his chest, then slowing, settling into a normal rhythm.

"I don't want to leave this boat," I say. "Ever."

It's true. Here, we're cozy, warm, *us*. Thick with the smell of sex, the heat of our bodies, and the love in our hearts. Everything feels so *natural*, so easy here.

But even our well-deserved postcoital bliss can't shake the cloud hanging over us. Because *outside*, it's cold and bitter and filled with unfriendly, hateful people who just don't *understand*.

Ben and Roland don't say anything to that, but I'm sure

they share my sentiment. There's still too much to talk about, too many decisions to make, and we're too exhausted. Ben lifts our hands and presses a kiss to the back of my fingers.

"Go to sleep, kitten," he tells me.

It's an order I'm too happy to obey.

9

BEN

I'm a schemer. Roland can attest to that. I've always been one, but my time spent in the British Army really cemented in the idea *don't go in without a plan*.

I have a plan. No. I *had* a plan. For tonight. But that's changed now.

I don't do well with change, and I can't shake it off. Rory's small body is tucked against me, so I carefully unwind her arms from my shoulders and guide her towards Roland instead. Her eyebrows knit, but her eyebrows don't open, and like a blind kitten she hunts for warmth, finds it in Roland's chest, and settles in there, going back to sleep.

Quietly, I climb out of the bunk. I pick my trousers off the floor, tug them on, and then grab my coat, throwing it over my naked chest. I won't be outside long. Just long enough to have a quick smoke and settle down the nerves bouncing around inside of me.

I open up the doors and climb out, making sure to shut them behind so I don't let the cold air in. It is frigid tonight, especially on the water, the fog making everything wet, making the cold crisper. I pull my coat tighter, pull out a cigarette, and light up. The tiny flame warms me from the inside out.

My eyes scan the horizon. Our friend the paparazzi isn't here anymore. I don't know why that disappoints me.

Maybe because I could use the distraction about now.

The plan was simple. Succinct. Perfect. Bring Rory and Roland over to my folks' for the first time. Have dinner. Celebrate the holidays. Then surprise them with a romantic night on a narrow boat off the Avon. And then…

When I put my pack of cigarettes back in my coat pocket, the backs of my fingers brush against it. A small, velvet box. I consider leaving it alone, but I must have a masochistic streak because my fingers pluck it out instead.

I hold it in the palm of my hand and pry its mouth open with my thumb so the box pops back on its own. Inside are two rings. A matching silver color, but one has a glittering diamond in the center of it, and the other is a thick band with smaller diamonds embedded in the rim.

His and hers engagement rings. One for Rory. One for Roland. Rings I planned to give them after I got down on a knee and proposed to them.

Like the bloody sap I am.

Not so long ago, when my sister told me she was pregnant with her first child, I was pissed. She was young then—too young. Her boyfriend was a cunt, and worst of all, they had no money to care for the kid. She *knew* how bad it was to grow up poor, yet she was going to make her child suffer the same fate. It was selfish and I told her as much.

Nearly cost us our relationship, me letting those words fly out of my mouth in anger. We got past it. Eventually. But by that point it'd already left a scar. And when her boyfriend left her and her money ran out, I didn't tell her I told her so. I was already working for Roland then, and the palace was giving me more money than I'd ever made in my life, so I paid the rent on her flat and gave her a monthly stipend until she got back on her feet.

She showed me up, in the end. She has two precious, beautiful nieces that I wouldn't trade anything for. She's a good mum, too. She made the best of a shit situation.

Rory is different. I know that. Rory has options my sister never had. She has *us*—but more than that, she has the palace. Helmsway Palace is not a place where children *want* for anything…Roland is proof of that.

I've gotten comfortable—maybe too comfortable—over this past year. Things with the three of us feel good. Feel right. It's easy when we're in our own world. It's easy when there aren't any consequences to our relationship.

But *easy* is safe, and safe isn't in the cards for me. Never was. I'd learned long ago to always look the gift horse in the mouth, but I'd gotten soft with them. Opened up. Let myself believe—in Rory's sappy, singsongy voice—that love really can conquer all.

Bloody joke, that.

I snap the box shut, put it away again, and let my gaze drift off with the river. I burn through one cigarette and then light another. By the time that one's dead, I've finally made a decision. One where there's no going back from. I crush the ashes against the side of the boat, flick the butt in the river, and then duck back inside.

ROLAND

J can't sleep when Ben isn't in bed with me.

I should be used to it by now—I could set my bloody watch by it. Every night, around 4:00 or 5:00 a.m., he'll get anxious. Then he'll get up and have to do something —he'll check on his lair, go to his office, or just go out to the porch and grab a smoke. Eventually, when I get tired of waiting up on him, I'll come find him and coax him back into bed like a stubborn sleepwalker.

I thought having Rory back, her body soft and warm beside me, would help me sleep through the night. But she doesn't. I can still feel Ben's absence, the cold spot in bed where he should be.

But I don't want to wake Rory—not after everything. So I hold her tighter and wait. It's maybe five or ten minutes before I hear the cabin doors shudder open and closed again. Then Ben's footsteps pad softly back in. When he's back with us, I catch a whiff of those Mayfairs he just can't quit.

"Heyo," I greet him as he sits up on the edge of the bed. But the second I see his face, I know something is wrong. His mouth is stuck in a tight, serious line, and his brown eyes are dark and contemplative.

"Can you wake Rory up?" he asks.

I slip my hand to her bare shoulder and press a line of kisses up the back of her neck. "Rory, love," I whisper.

She groans, curls her body into me, and her eyes blink open sleepily. "Whassit?"

"I've been thinking," Ben says, and the deep intensity of his tone seems to jerk her out of her fog. She props herself up on her elbow, refocusing on him.

"Dangerous habit," I say, but Ben cuts me a sharp look. It's not the time for levity, apparently. I shut my mouth.

Ben doesn't preamble or wind around the subject the way Rory does. Instead, he just comes out with it. "You need to get married. The two of you."

Now it's Rory's turn to narrow her eyes, her mouth thinning. They're both incredibly passionate, stubborn people, so I attempt to temper the oncoming onslaught with a simple "Perhaps this is a more complicated conversation for another time..."

"No," Rory says firmly. "We can have it now. I'm not marrying Roland."

I can't say why—but that hurts.

"Well. Good talk," I mumble.

"*Yes*, it is," Ben counters. "Look—I'm not an idiot. I love you Rory, very much. And you too, Roland. But we knew something like this could happen. One of us would have to make a choice. And I've made it. What we have is special, but..."

"*But?*" When Rory says it, it comes out shocked. "There are no *buts*. I'm not interested in anything that divides us, Ben—you of all people should know that. We agreed—it's the three of us or nothing."

"But it's *not* the three of us anymore," Ben argues. "It's the four of us. We have to be realistic. I can't give the baby a throne. I can't give him the same privileges that a life of royalty will. I grew up poor, and in a family that struggled for every pound. I'm not going to leave my child to the same fate." His eyes meet mine suddenly. "Roland, back me up on this."

Rory turns to me, too, and I feel pinned. Ben is the brain —cold, hard, steely logic. He's made a pros and cons list, done the calculations, and come up with a black-and-white answer without any wiggle room. Rory...she's close to tears now. She's all heart, and I can see it spilling, aching, hurting inside of her...because a union with only two of us doesn't *feel* right.

And now, the two sides are looking to me for an answer. My tongue feels trapped to the roof of my mouth. I want to take them both in my arms, kiss them, and remind them that none of this matters, that our love is the most important.

But the worst part is…

I know he's right.

A bastard doesn't get a shot at the crown. But an *heir*…

"Ben isn't wrong," I say, and the words sound hollow, even as I try to soften them out. "If we got married...and I claimed this child for my own...he could be the next king of England."

It's a terrible thing to watch—the way any trace of hope just falls off Rory's face. This is not how I imagined a proposal would go. Instead of devotions of love and loyalty, there's heartbreak. A fracture in our beautiful world.

"This *can't* be the only way," Rory insists, reaching out and grabbing Ben's hand, tugging him closer. "I'm not letting you go. And, frankly, I'm pissed that you're so willing to walk away from this."

Now the hardness in Ben's face cracks. He cups Rory's face and reassures her. "No...that's not it. I will *always* be your boyfriend." His eyes meet mine, those dark orbs so intense and full of love that I want to kiss him. "And yours." Then he turns to Rory again and adds, "But this baby needs to be a Pennington. And so do you."

"I love you" tumbles out of Rory's lips, over and over, with heartbreaking sincerity. "I love you, I love you…"

"I love you, too," Ben calms her, and he kisses her gently.

He locks eyes with me—and we don't say it, because we know—but I grab the back of his head and I kiss him, deep and hard, because even though he says I won't, I feel him pulling away, and suddenly I can't get close enough to him.

"Thank you," I murmur breathlessly when we break apart, even though it feels like a rotten thing to thank someone for but, but it feels like something that needs to be said.

"I'd do anything for you," Ben says.

He means it. I know he means it.

I'd do anything for him, too. And for Rory.

The baby changes everything. We share kisses, and tears, and finally all pile up together again, until we can't tell whose limbs belong to whom. I haven't prayed in a damn long time, but once they've both fallen asleep and all I can hear is their mirrored breaths and the water lapping the side of the boat, quietly, to myself, I pray that the three of us can survive this.

RORY

*W*e try to make it a happy occasion.

Roland proposes to me a second time—since the first wasn't so much a proposal as it was a conscious decision made by the three of us. This time, Roland and I are at a restaurant, in the public eye, and there are cameras around to take our pictures. The media goes into a frenzy about us—Rory and Roland, enjoying their engagement. Roland and Rory, picking out wedding cake. Roland and Rory, the flashback edition, and the scandalous sex tape that started it all. Roland and Rory, the cutest thing since baby ducks learned to cross the street single file.

There's no mention of Ben anymore. Everyone seems to have forgotten the kiss he and Roland shared at Roland's swearing-in ceremony. They seem to have forgotten Ben entirely.

Ben insists that it's okay—he hates being in the public eye anyway. He insists that he's happy for us. That it's better this way. But he's spending more time in his office, skipping out on date nights because he has "too much work," and he's upped his cigarette consumption to nearly a pack a day.

It's killing him. It's killing *me*. But Maddie's voice keeps tumbling through my head—

Sacrifice. She'd warned me, hadn't she? We all have to make sacrifices for our children. And every day this baby grows, I know one thing for sure: that this little life is the most important thing in the world to me and I would do anything for it.

And there are worse sacrifices to make than marrying the love of your life.

There are parts of it that really aren't so bad—parts of it that are *fun*, actually. We've kept a tight grip on most of the PR that's going out around the wedding, leaking only bits and pieces of information here and there. Roland has a reporter he trusts, an American journalist by the name of Santiago Price, who is known, apparently, for his gaudy and bizarre celebrity spreads, so he grants the man an exclusive pre-royal-wedding photoshoot.

I'm expecting a stuffy, prom-style scenario, with white gloves and rubbery smiles while a man tells us to say *cheers* before he snaps the photo, and for a while, that's what it is. They want a few of the whole (remaining) royal family in one frame, so Queen Selena joins us. It's hard for me to describe the queen of England; even though I've been dating her son for over a year now and I live in the same palace as she does, I barely know the woman. She reminds me very much of a swan: cold, beautiful, and utterly detached from everything and everyone around her. The only person that makes her light up is her beloved son, Roland, and even he doesn't get a free pass from her.

They have her dressed in a beautiful, single-shoulder white dress that hugs her slim frame. It has a filigree design that climbs her thigh, exposing bits of her pale skin around the curves of the flowers. Her blonde hair cascades perfectly around her shoulders. She is—in layman's terms—England's favorite MILF. Meanwhile, I'm in a dress that is supposed to suggest *wedding attire*, a white gown that poofs around my hips. I'm actually grateful for the extra *poof*, since I'm only three months in and, already, my belly is starting to round.

Selena and I are in matching colors, I guess, purposefully —the two most important women in Roland's life. But I feel like a cupcake, and she looks like Aphrodite herself.

We're sitting in the sitting room, which, from what I can tell, is a place to do just that—sit. There's a grand piano, a birdcage, and a rolling bar, but the three of us sit on one of the large sofas as we wait for the cameras to finish setting up.

This also happens to be the room I first made love to Roland in, in front of the entire world, with my camera phone accidentally rolling. There's something full circle about it. Which...I'm trying not to think about with Roland's mother sitting only a couple feet away from me. Roland is handsome as a fox in his silver suit, his hair pushed to the side, the edges trimmed down to give him a sleek, modern look. They're handing out champagne to get us loose to the photos (I keep making up creative excuses not to take one), and Roland is sipping his second—maybe third—flute of the evening.

Queen Selena reaches out and her fingertips grace a passing assistant. "Excuse me," she says, her voice a cougar's purr, "would you be so kind as to steal one of the makeup artists for me? Rory needs a little touch-up around the eyes. We want her to look like a princess for goodness' sake, not one of the living dead."

"Yes, Your Majesty," the woman says before fluttering off to follow her orders.

Selena turns to me, purses her lips in a smile, and winks, as though she's done me some huge favor by insulting the bags around my eyes. "Don't worry," she tells me. "I'll look out for you."

I'm half-tempted to tell her I wouldn't look so tired if I wasn't up banging her son all night, but that's not the sort of thing a princess says and I'm supposed to be *princessly* now, so I try on a smile. "Thank you," I say politely.

"Of course," she chimes. "We're family now, after all."

The reminder feels like lead in my stomach. The dress bunches up in all the wrong places, my feet feel tight in these heels, I'm hungry even though we just ate lunch, and I'm aching to vanish down some hidden staircase and order a boatload of Chinese food. Not just any Chinese food, either —New York, hole-in-the-wall Chinese food. The problem about being a traveler, I've discovered, is that my cravings come from all across the globe…and it's not like I can get Roland to just jet off to Brooklyn and grab me a spring roll.

I turn to Roland, who's perched on the arm of the sofa. The boy can't follow the rules long enough to sit in a chair properly, so I know he's feeling the pain of being well-behaved.

"You're making that drink look good," I murmur to him.

He chuckles. "Too bad you're…"

My eyes go wide. I know he's had a couple flutes of champagne, but he is *not* that drunk. He's not drunk enough to blab to everyone that I'm pregnant, even though the three of us agreed we wouldn't tell anyone until *after* the wedding ceremony. There's enough scandal surrounding us as it is.

He must see the fear in my eyes, because the words die on his tongue. Instead, he fumbles with a "…you know," and then finishes gracefully by tapping the tip of my nose with his finger and making a "boop" sound.

"What does she know?" Selena interjects. She's quick on the uptake, and truthfully, I'm amazed that she hasn't figured out I'm pregnant already. I don't know—maybe she has. The way she glares at me out of the corners of her eyes sometimes, I wonder.

"He means it's too bad I can't drink because I'm on a cleanse," I spit out quickly with a smile. "You know. Alcohol. Empty calories. I have to fit in my dress somehow, right?"

"Quite," the queen says sharply, but she's eyeing us suspiciously. She knows we're up to something—even if she hasn't guessed the *what* of it yet.

We get touched up, poked, and prodded, until finally Santiago, a bald man in a purple velvet blazer, begins flashing his camera around us. He directs us to look up, down, smile —*my prince, put your arm around the girl—you are young! You are in love! Sí, sí, magnífico!*

It's all overwhelming and as soon as the camera starts going off, it's like I've forgotten how to smile. I work my mouth into an upturned shape, show some teeth, and hope they can plaster someone else's smile on my face in editing. Anything, I'm certain, would be better than the forced jacko'-lantern grin I've got going on.

Selena and Roland, of course, are pros at this; she's used to being in front of the camera, and Roland can't help but ooze charm. After maybe thirty minutes of this, Selena's assistant steps into frame and dips down so she can whisper something in Selena's ear. Selena nods, then turns to everyone, blasts a smile, and says, "Right. I'm done here. Thank you for your time, Mr. Price."

With that, she stands only long enough for them to take the pins out of her dress, then simply walks out. The joys of being queen, I guess. When she's done, *she's done*, and no one can tell her otherwise.

Once his mother is out of earshot, Roland gives my shoulder a squeeze and asks, "Care to shake things up?"

"Shake up *how*?" I ask and lean against him. "Like… naptime and second lunch in bed?"

He crinkles his nose. "Mm, I'm thinking more along the lines of…*getting wild*. You know. Embrace our animal nature. Give in to carnality. You, Jane, me, Tarzan."

I make a noise that's half a scoff, half a laugh. "What are you talking about—? *Oh!*"

My breath catches in my throat when I see it. Roland

grins and pushes off the sofa, jumping to his feet. "Finally, the man of the hour!" he announces and steps over to a man holding a black-and-white capuchin monkey. Then he turns to the monkey. "Cyril, is it? It's a pleasure to meet you, buddy."

Then Roland lifts out his hand, and the monkey, *Cyril*, climbs up his trainer's arm, perches on his wrist, and uses both his tiny hands to grab Roland's big one, shaking it.

It's so cute, the noise that leaves my throat is an inhumane squeal, and I clasp my hand over my mouth so I don't accidentally break the glass windows with my piercing octave.

Roland then shakes the trainer's hand, and they talk a little bit, the trainer going through a number of *Your Highness* remarks, and I'm trying to listen, but I can't stop staring, slack-jawed, and this *monkey in Helmsway Palace*.

He's small and hunched over, the size of my head, maybe, with black fur and a white, heart-shaped face. Cyril has a hand on his trainer's arm, clinging to the other man, but only for balance—he's looking around the room boldly, curiously. Cyril the monkey doesn't seem incredibly impressed by the portrait of the late king in the corner or the Mandarin rug on the wall, but he does fix his eyes on the canaries fluttering around in their cage and lets out a low, intrigued trill.

I love him. My heart can't handle this.

"Rory!" Roland grins and sweeps his arm, motioning me over. "C'mere, meet our guest."

I haven't been this shy since my first celebrity sighting (Joel Madden à la Good Charlotte fame—I was the most starstruck teen in Jamba Juice). I lift myself slowly from the couch and approach the three of them.

"Oh my God..." I murmur. "Are you sure he's real?"

I've never been this close to a monkey. I've seen them in the zoo, sure, but not *like this*.

The trainer laughs. "He's real, all right," the man says, a strong Australian accent bleeding out. "Famous, too."

"Famous?" I echo.

"That's right. Have you seen *Die Fast* or *Maggie's Mischief?* He's in both of those. We spend a lot of time in Hollywood doing gigs there—just came from one, actually. Still under wraps, though; we can't say much about it."

As if he knows we're talking about him, Cyril suddenly lets out a screech. "Sorry, he's a little testy blighter," his trainer mumbles. "Haven't had his snack yet."

He pulls out a small plastic baggy with orange slices in it and picks one out, handing it over to Cyril. The monkey takes it in his small hands and starts quickly nibbling into it, making happy little cooing sounds.

"Roland…" I grip his arm and turn to him. "Why did you borrow a monkey from Hollywood?"

Confusion flashes across his eyes. "Because I wanted to."

And for Roland, there will never be a better answer. He wants it, he gets it. And, I guess, so do I, now that I'm the soon-to-be princess.

I've got to admit, if monkeys on demand are perks of the position, maybe, just *maybe*, I'm starting to warm up to the idea of being British royalty. I feel like a little girl at Christmas, bouncing up and down excitedly on my toes. "Can I hold him?"

"Step right up." Roland slips his hand to my back and guides me closer. I lean against him, feeling incredibly safe folded against his body. The trainer hands me a cashew nut and shows me how to entice Cyril over to my arm with it.

The monkey climbs over me boldly, and I can't help the yelp of delight that escapes me. His little hands and feet cling like cat paws, but he's so light as he scampers down my arm to take the nut. He holds it in his tiny fingers, and his body vibrates with delight as he chews it.

My heart tightens in my chest. He's so precious, I can't handle it. "I think I'm in love," I tell Roland.

"You better not be trying to steal my girl, mate." Roland wags his finger at Cyril. The monkey wraps both hands around Roland's finger, and they're so small, I want to cry. Oh, no—I *am* crying. I can't help it, something about that image breaks something inside of me. I know it's a monkey, but…all I can think about is how, soon, Roland's going to be a father, and there's going to be a *baby* hand reaching for his. I can see it suddenly, and my heart is swelling ten times its normal size.

"Rory." Roland's voice is suddenly thick with concern, and he wraps his arm around my middle. "Are you okay?"

"Yes." I smile, quickly pushing back the tears. I slip my hand in his and squeeze it as I rest it over my belly…over our baby, growing inside of me.

Cyril sneezes and licks any trace of cashew from my fingers, and I'm laughing again.

Hormones, man. They're a bitch.

I've completely forgotten about the cameras, but now they're on us in full force. Santiago takes control, orchestrating the two of us and Cyril. The Royal Circus is the theme, apparently, and we're having fun with it. Cyril is a good sport, jumping around my shoulders, taking up poses for the camera, and yanking on Roland's hair.

We've been at it for almost half an hour when I take Roland by the chin and pull him into a kiss. "Thank you," I say.

"What for?"

"Reminding me how insanely fun life is with you."

A warm grin spreads over Roland's mouth. "Rory…I will spend the rest of my life making sure every day with you is an adventure. I can promise you that."

Out of the corner of my eye, I catch a stalker in the hallway. Ben peeks in the doorway, and his eyebrows fly up his forehead when he sees the chaos.

"Ben!" I cry out. "Come join us!"

But Ben's body goes stiff when he sees Cyril. "No, thank you."

"What...not afraid of a monkey, are you, mate?" Roland teases.

"It's a wild animal loose in the palace," Ben states flatly.

"You know—" Roland catches Cyril's face gently in his hand. "—I think you two look quite alike, don't you think?"

Ben scowls. He's about to leave, so I rush over and grab his arm, dragging him into the room. "Just say hi...it's only polite!"

Reluctantly, Ben finally loosens his feet and follows me. "How sentient is it?" he asks, eyeing Cyril suspiciously.

"He's a monkey, not Skynet," I correct him.

"Right, but...should I...use sign language? How does he communicate?"

"With these." I hold up a cashew and hand it over to Ben. "Just give him one."

Ben puts the cashew in his palm and holds it up as an offering to Cyril, who is sitting on Roland's shoulder. Cyril glances up at Ben, then plucks up the cashew. He puts it in his mouth, then leaps over to Ben, grabbing on to his shirt. Ben looks momentarily startled, but when the monkey just clutches him, he adjusts his blazer to cradle the little guy in it.

"What have you monsters done to him?" Ben says.

"Nothing!" I protest. But there's no denying it—there's something about Ben that makes *everyone* instantly feel safer. Even the monkey gets it.

I wrap my arm around my boys—one arm around Ben's shoulders, the other around Roland. "Smile!" I tell them and add, "We need a family photo."

This feels right now. The three of us. Together.

The photoshoot finally winds down; Cyril is yawning, showing off his monkey teeth. We thank him.

Before Cyril leaves, however, he glances at his trainer,

who motions to him in sign language. Then the monkey climbs up the back of my dress (the sensation of tiny hands on my back does not get less strange), hops onto my shoulder, and plants a kiss on my cheek.

My mouth drops open in surprise, and a laugh bubbles up from my chest.

"Cheeky monkey," Ben mutters.

"I love him," I whine.

Roland comes up behind me—I feel his hands over my hips first, then his arms ensnare me and he pulls me up against him. "Do you want him? We could buy him, probably."

"No," I sigh wistfully as I watch Cyril leave on the shoulder of his trainer. "Our love burned too brightly too quick. It would never last."

"A true Shakespearian tragedy," Roland murmurs.

My gaze falls to Ben, who is crossing his arms over his chest. His body posture is squaring off again, already on the defense now that Cyril isn't the center of everyone's attention.

I slip out of Roland's embrace and tug on Ben's shoulder. "Ben—help me out of this, please?" I bat my eyes and pull the fabric of my dress.

His jaw sets, but he can't say no to me. He nods instead. "All right."

BEN

*R*ory's moods have been fluctuating from one extreme to the other, and it's only partially due to the change in hormones.

This wedding has put stress on all of us. Some days, it feels like we might crack under the weight of it. Other days, it brings us closer, and we ravage each other as if each time might be our last.

Today is a good day. Rory's in a good mood.

She's smiling, laughing, practically skipping around the palace. I'll put up with a monkey just to see her smile. I will *steal* that monkey if that's what it takes.

There's not a lot of privacy in this room, but they've set up a small "dressing area" to the side. A silk-screen room divider separates Rory's pile of clothes from the rest of it, and I follow her behind the divider.

Rory is a lot of things, but shy isn't one of them. She turns so I can unzip her dress and, as soon as I do, she shimmies out of it and kicks it to the side.

"Good lord," she sighs. "That is so much better. I feel twenty pounds lighter."

I'm trying not to stare at her as she is, nearly naked. My

gaze follows her ginger hair, which falls in thick rivulets down her shoulders, to her bra, cupping her swollen breasts. Her tummy has a little extra roundness to it, the start of a baby bump, and there's something about it that I find incredibly attractive on some base, animalistic level. Teal boy shorts hug the curve of her arse and her luscious thighs—and now she's caught me looking.

I clear my throat and turn my eyes to the wall instead, watching our shadows.

She laughs and, in the corner of my vision, I see her grab her jeans and yank them up her hips. "You're my boyfriend, Ben. You're allowed to look."

"Right, well. Time and a place." *And if I keep looking, I'm going to want to touch, and there's only so much the divider can hide.*

"Always doing the *proper* thing, aren't you? Don't you get tired of it?"

My jaw tightens. "One of us has to follow the rules."

She's shuffling around, and I can see her flurry of motion, but she's taken a step back and it's hard to make out the details.

Then I feel her. Her hands slide down my waist and she hooks her thumbs into the pockets my trousers. She's a good head shorter than me, so I know she must be standing on her tippy-toes when the warmth of her breath hits the back of my neck.

"Hey, Ben?" she says, her voice airy and innocent.

"Yes?"

Her teeth find my earlobe and she gives it a little nibble before purring, "*Bagsy.*"

I can't help it—a shudder travels through me, and my blood rushes to my prick, making it swell against the confines of my trousers. I swallow. Hard. She's done the impossible—caught the bodyguard off guard—and now my words stick in my throat.

Her plump lips press a single kiss under my ear. "Meet me in Roland's room in thirty?"

"Sure." I want my tone to smoothen out, but instead it has all the vibration of a growl.

"Perfect." I can feel her grin against my neck. "Oh, and ummm…you might want to take the hidden staircase behind the fireplace. You know…" Her nimble fingers walk down my trousers and trace the increasingly visible outline of my erection. "…so you don't traumatize the monkey."

"Anything else?"

"Mmm…oh! Bring your rope, please, sir."

Rory trying to be coy is equal parts adorable and sexy; it makes my heart and cock ache. She presses a final kiss to the back of my neck and then skips out from behind the divider to join everyone else. And…leaves me throbbing.

"Shit," I mutter under my breath.

My eyes fall to the fireplace, which is half on my side of the divider.

The palace certainly has its secrets. And I know all of them.

I touch a lever disguised as a candleholder and a hidden door clicks open. It's blended into the square wooden paneling in the wall. I open it the rest of the way and slip out through the staircase.

I vanish completely, and the camera crew is none the wiser.

13

RORY

$\mathcal{I}$t doesn't take much to convince Roland to step away.

He must see a mischievous twinkle in my eyes, because he hooks an arm around my shoulder and says, "What're you up to, then, March?"

I tell him. He is, of course, in.

I don't think there's ever a time when Roland *isn't* horny, honestly. His sex drive is just as bad, if not worse, than mine.

Even though each of us technically have our own bedrooms at the palace, Roland's room has pretty much become our room. Unsurprisingly, besides the queen's room (which I've only ever seen through a crack in the doorway in passing), Prince Roland has the best room in the palace. Wooden paneled walls, a gas-lit fireplace, shelves stacked with well-read books, and of course, the bed fit for a king— huge, soft, with an olive-colored comforter and plush pillows. What I'm *really* interested in right now is the head-board, an ornate, wooden thing with swirls and slots engraved in it.

When we get there, Ben is already there, sitting on the edge of the bed, waiting patiently. As promised, his "play rope"—cotton soft and handwoven—sits on the bed beside him, wound up in a neat coil.

"Took you long enough," he says, but I don't think he means it. Personally, I think Ben just *loves* complaining. It's easier to complain than to admit he's actually having fun.

Unfortunately for him, I never let him stay grumpy for long. I skip over, straddle his lap, and run my fingers through his short hair, down to the prickly bits on the nape of his neck. "You know how this place is. You take one wrong turn and end up in Narnia."

He's biting back a smile. "Is that so?"

"Mmhm. Tumnus says hi."

I nibble at his lower lip. When he leans forward to kiss me, however, I shrug away coyly. "Is that for me?" I ask, glancing at the rope.

"Yes."

Ben reaches for it. And—I should preface—this is Ben's *thing*. He loves tying me and Roland up. Growing up—he's told me—he spent a couple of summers working as a dock boy and got incredibly good at sailor's knots. But he doesn't tie boats to docks anymore; instead, he'll use his knots to anchor me to the bedpost, leaving me helpless and at his mercy.

I have something different in mind for tonight, though. Before he can grab it, I tiptoe my fingers to the rope and tug it away from him. "Or…I was thinking…we could switch it up."

Ben's thick eyebrows knit the realization hits him. "No," he says.

I pout. "You don't even know what I *want*."

"Yes, I do. You want to tie me down."

Roland flops down on the bed beside us. "Don't you trust us, mate?"

"Yes," Ben says, flustered. "But…"

But he's not accustomed to not being the one in control.

If it's something he's uncomfortable with, obviously, I'm not going to push him. But I also want him to know that he can trust us as much as we trust him. "So…is this a hard limit or a soft limit?" I ask.

I'm not ashamed to admit I cheat here a little—I "adjust" in my seat, using the opportunity to grid my pelvis against his lap. I feel his erection press back against me—*c'mon*, Ben, we both know you're warming to the idea—and a small growl escapes him.

"If I say release me," he yields finally, "you release me."

"Of course." I grin. "You're the sadist. Not me."

Maybe as one last play for dominance, Ben catches my throat in his hand and kisses me roughly. I gasp in his mouth as the air leaves my lungs, making me dizzy and aroused, melting like butter in his lap.

Roland breaks the spell, slipping his hand up my thigh while kissing the base of Ben's neck. And just like that, I remember that I have a job to do. I slip my hand to Ben's wrist, and he removes his fingers from my throat. I dangle the rope and say, "No more stalling. Shirt off, Tolle."

Ben frowns at that, but he does unbutton his shirt and pushes it off his shoulders, tossing it to the side. I climb off him and point to the bed. "Lie down. Arms up."

"Bossy," he says, but I can tell by the crinkle of his eyes that he's amused. Kitten is trying her hand at lioness. He kicks off his shoes and socks and then shifts to the center of the bed, lying down on his back. His arms drop loosely over his head.

I pick up the rope and sit on the pillow beside him. I thread the rope through the slots in the headboard and then wrap the ends around his wrists. When Ben does this, he makes it look easy. Elegant. The only thing I know how to tie is my shoes, so I find myself wrapping the rope randomly around his wrists and the headboard.

Ben clears his throat. "The rabbit goes through the hole…"

"Shut up!" I say as I fight with the rope. "I've got this!"

Eventually, I tie his arms to the bed in—well. It's not really a knot? But the rope is so jumbled up, it'll probably take a chainsaw to break him loose.

"How is that?" I ask. "Not too tight?"

"No," he says. He's calm. Reassuring.

Roland doesn't waste time playing, though. He traces his fingertips down the excruciatingly perfect lines of Ben's toned body, thumbing one of Ben's hard nipples before running his finger down the center of Ben, drawing ovals around his abdomen. "Can you break free?" Roland asks. His reaches Ben's belt, which he undoes.

Ben tries to pull his wrists from the headboard, and I hold my breath, but the rope doesn't let him go far. "No."

"Perfect."

Roland's lips meet Ben's hip, and his hand slides down Ben's pants. Ben groans, his head falling back. Ben takes care of us so much, it's not often we get to reciprocate. I flick one of his nipples, enjoying the way it makes him shudder, and cover his strong chest and abdomen in sweet, butterfly kisses. We take our time, worshipping him, and eventually, the stiffness in Ben's shoulders melts. He's giving in to it, finally, letting us take care of him, and he lets out a small sigh.

"You're perfect, do you know that?" I tell him.

"So are you," he responds.

I'm buzzing. He turns me on so much that, every time I rub my thighs together, I can feel my soaked panties. I need him. I push my panties down my legs and kick them off before I move to straddle Ben's chest. His dark eyes connect with mine, and he looks like he wants to devour me…and I suddenly feel so sexy and so powerful.

I take them hem of my dress and, slowly, I draw it up my

thighs. I give him a little flash of my pussy and then ask, "Do you want to taste?"

He wets his lips. "Yes."

Then Roland comes behind me. I feel his large hands move to the sides of my dress, and he pulls it up, yanking it off my body, over my head. He pops my bra off next, so now I'm completely naked and on display. "How much?" Roland asks. He kisses my neck and nibbles my earlobe, which makes me sigh with pleasure. His hands slip up my body and cup my breasts, caressing them, and I find myself pushing into his hands, loving his touch.

"Fuck," Ben swears. I feel him jerk underneath me as he tries his restraints again—but no luck. I've knotted him up tightly. His eyes flash with longing as his gaze fixes on Roland fondling me…just out of reach.

"That's not an answer," Roland responds.

"I want to taste her. More than anything." His voice is husky, thick with lust.

"You heard him, kitten." Roland's hands leave my chest and instead move to my hips, urging me forward.

Carefully, I climb forward so I'm straddling Ben's face. I have to grip the headboard to brace myself. I feel his hot breath beating against my damp sex first. Then I move my hand down and part my lips before lowering myself down. I'm expecting it, but I still find myself gasping sharply with surprise when his tongue flicks over my sensitive skin. He feels so wet, so warm, so *good*, and I moan and arch against his mouth as he captures me completely. I feel his moan vibrate through me, sending shock waves of pleasure through me that are so intense, my nipples instantly go pebble hard and my fingers tighten their grip.

Even tied down, there is nothing submissive about Ben. He's taking his time with me, working me up at his pace. He tastes my lips, gently nibbles my stiff nub, and teases my greedy entrance. Every flick of his tongue sends me to the heights of ecstasy, and I shove my hand into his hair, holding him tightly against me, *needing* him so badly. He slows when he can tell I'm getting close, denying me the release I want more than anything, until I'm panting, throbbing, my legs trembling.

I'm grinding on his lips, aching, when I feel a body behind me. Roland presses against me, his knees on either side of Ben. His hand slips over my hip, down the curve of my ass, and he kisses my neck at that sweet spot right under my jaw. Here, he murmurs, "Lift your hips, kitten."

So I do—even though it's painful to remove them from Ben's mouth. But then I feel him—the thick head of Roland pressing against me. Roland eases inside of me and fills me. Between my arousal and Ben's saliva, I'm soaking wet, and he slips in me easily. I gasp and my palm hits the wall. Roland starts to fuck me and I lose my grip. My knees slip, forcing them wide. My clit falls right on Ben's waiting mouth. Before I know it, I'm bent over, clinging to the wall, while Roland pounds into me from behind, each thrust rubbing my swollen clit over Ben's greedy tongue.

I whimper, and both their names fall from my lips, with a rapid succession of "Oh God, *oh my God*!" It feels so good—too good—and there's absolutely nothing I can do to slow down the onslaught of pleasure…nor do I want to. I let it overwhelm me until I'm quivering, everything in me tight and teetering on the verge of collapse.

My orgasm hits me before I know it. I cry out, gripping Ben's hair so tightly I feel like I might rip it from his skull, but he doesn't mind; he just attacks my clit more voraciously with his tongue. Roland pumps himself deeply inside of me, fucking me through my intense orgasm, until he falls over the edge, too, swearing as he shoots inside of me. And Ben— he moans, sucking and licking us both up.

I'm boneless, my limbs like jelly when Roland finally pries me off Ben, slips out of me, and lays me down beside him.

My thighs feel stuck in this position, spread apart sluttishly, and Roland gives me a heated kiss as he pets me between my legs, teasing out the last throbs. It feels so good, I'm almost crying.

Then Roland—ravenous—shifts from me to kiss Ben. Ben's lips are swollen, his mouth and beard glistening with me. As Roland laps him clean, Ben lets out an agonized noise and his hips lift wantingly. His pants are only partially down his hips still, but Roland reaches down and tugs his cock free, and I wet my lips at the sight of him. He's rock hard, beet red with need, and he's dripped arousal down the side of his perfect cock, leaving a mess on his belly. Roland doesn't tease —Roland knows what he wants and he takes it. I watch with dry-throated awe as he wraps his fingers tightly around Ben's cock and yanks him, fingers moving swiftly up and down.

Ben's so worked up, it doesn't take long.

Ben lift his hips into Roland's hand as his release comes in thick, ropey torrents. Ben tosses his head back, fights his binds so hard they look red on his skin, and he lets out a string of swears. He's not finished until Roland has massaged every last drop from him, and only then does he finally start to wilt.

Roland's violet eyes meet mine then. "Kitten," he says, his voice a low purr. "You know what you have to do."

I do. A kitten's work is never done. Obediently, I crawl down and dip my head to lap up the streams of white shot across Ben's abdomen. The sensation of my tongue draws a fresh groan from him and he twitches, so I lap that up, too, the saltiness at the tip of his cock, until he's completely clean. But I'm greedy for it now, hungry for his sweet taste. I tickle the dark curls on his pelvis and slip my hand lower, under-neath, rubbing the tight sac there. I take my time rolling my tongue over the tip of him and wrapping my lips around it and sucking, until I feel him throb between my lips and taste a little more, leaking into my mouth.

Finally Ben chokes out a half-pleasured, half-pained "Enough. Please."

So I listen to his limits and release him—like I said I would. I press small kisses to his abdomen instead and kiss up his stomach, his chest. I kiss his lips, finally, and he sighs with relief into my mouth—as though his orgasm was good, but my kiss is better. As we kiss, Roland gets to work undoing Ben's binds…or trying to, at least.

"Bloody hell," he finally says, "What'd you do here?"

I shrug. "Whoops." I trace my finger down Ben's chest and grin. "I guess you're stuck here."

Ben grunts. "I don't think I could survive it. You two would eat me alive."

"You'd love it," Roland counters.

It takes both me and Roland, but finally, we manage to undo Ben. He sits up and rubs his wrists.

"So?" I ask. "What'd you think?"

His eyes flash to me. "I think," he says, "you're in trouble now, kitten."

I squeal with delight as he catches my lips in a deep, loving, dominant kiss.

14

ROLAND

*W*e're all so exhausted, we sleep well past breakfast.

For once, I'm the first one up. Usually Ben beats me to it, but I figured he could use the rest. He's got a face full of Rory's wild ginger curls, but he doesn't seem to mind; he sleeps on soundlessly, his arm around her middle. I kiss the top of Ben's head, then reach across from him to kiss Rory's. Extracting myself from Ben without waking him up is a near-impossible task, but somehow, I manage it.

I'm awake, I had some of the best sex of my life last night, and I'm in a damned good mood. I want to spoil my loves with breakfast in bed—my personal favorite activity. If it were up to me, we'd never leave the bed; our days would be spent shagging, our nights cuddling, and we'd only ever get up to use the loo or take an occasional shower.

I spent so much of my life longing to leave the palace, and now I crave lazy days in.

I don't bother with clothes. I have a terry cloth robe with my initials on it, so I sling it over my shoulders and tie it off at the middle. I exit our room, quietly shutting the door behind me. I greet the guards posted at my door, then saunter off to the dining room to see what's left of breakfast.

Technically, we have two dining rooms—one for formal events and major guests, and one for the day-to-day nonsense of life. This is the latter, a cozy dayroom with long windows to let in the morning light, eggshell-blue walls, a piano that I enjoy tinkering with now and then. I see the table stacked with trays of biscuits, scones, poached eggs, fried tomatoes and mushrooms, toast, sausages, and on and on. I clear off one of the pastry trays and start to make three separate plates. Rory's favorite is bacon and carbs, Ben enjoys eggs, and I pick at a little bit of everything.

The side doors click open and I glance up to see a familiar face.

"Your Highness, I've kept some fresh scones warm in the oven, if you'd prefer." Miss Thompson is a stout, older woman who runs the kitchen. She's one of the many staff members in the palace who essentially raised me from a pup —after my father passed away, all I had to care for me was my mum, and she wasn't always the warmest. I credit much of my upbringing to women like Miss Thompson, who endured my endless questions, my teenage angst, and gave me a spoon and said, "Taste this, it'll make you feel better."

"Miss Thompson," I greet her, "you know me too well. What would I do without you?"

"You'd suffer cold scones, I imagine." She gives me a wink and then slips back out the doors she came from to grab my scones.

"You know," my mum remarks, glaring at my tray, "that's how we get mice."

And good lord—I didn't even see her there. She's finished breakfast, of course, up with the sun, and she's sitting in the corner of the room by the piano, reading a book and enjoying a cup of tea.

Well. *Sipping*, at least. I'm not so certain my mother, the queen of England, *enjoys* much of anything.

"I'll make them lick up the crumbs," I tell her.

Her face doesn't budge. I've got no idea whether it's the Botox or if she truly has her emotion on lockdown. Probably a little bit of both, I'd say. "Roland, dear. Won't you have a cup of tea with me?"

It's phrased as a question, but it's not a question—it's a command. I'm feeling too high, and I don't want to test her temper, not this early in the morning, so I oblige. When Miss Thompson comes back, I ask her if I can bother her for a cup and she complies, pouring me some tea. I take the seat across from mum—a plush armchair—and blow on the hot tea before taking a swallow.

"The wedding is coming up quickly," she comments. There's no affectation to her voice, positive or negative.

"Mm," I respond. "I suppose it is."

And then she gets straight to the point: "I don't know what arrangement the three of you have struck up—and I certainly don't want to know. I don't think the rest of the world should, either. Some things…should remain sacred. Private."

"Secret, you mean," I correct her.

She knows how to sail through ripples in a conversation like a duck through water. "All that to say…I think you've made the right choice." She places her hand on my chair. My mother was never the touchy-feely type; I could probably count on one hand the amount of times she's hugged me. She was raising a future king after all, not a son. But now, the tips of her fingers just brush the top of my hand, which is the equivalent to a real, ten-second bear hug from her. "I know I've had my doubts about Rory in the past. And I know it must have been hard for you to make the choice. But I'm *proud* of you for making it—and I'm proud of you for marrying her."

Her words feel a bit like a Trojan horse—a pretty package wrapping up something ugly. At the same time…I'll admit it. It's nice to hear her say she's proud of me.

With my father gone and my aunt in prison, my mum is all the family I have. We haven't always seen eye to eye, and especially not where it comes to Rory.

But she's making an effort. And that counts for something with me.

I take her hand in mine and give it a light squeeze. "Thank you, Mum."

She pulls her lips in a tight smile. "You'll make a proper king," she tells me, "when the time comes." Then she retracts her hand from my hold. I've used my minutes of affection for the day.

Which is fine. I've run out of things to say.

We could be strangers these days, the two of us.

"I better get on," I say, "before the scones gets cold again."

She says nothing; she simply turns away from me and goes back to her book.

I pile up the kettle along with my plates onto a tray to take back to the bedroom. I've got no idea what kind of father I'll be; my father died when I was young, and my memories of him are distant and fragmented. But one thing is for sure…

I'm going to hug my damn kid. A lot. All the time. Every chance I get.

15

RORY

They say that if you want something, you have to
envision it.

But I'm standing in front of a mirror, watching myself get
poked in a wedding gown, and I'm still not sure I really *want*
this.

The dress—don't get me wrong—is undeniably beautiful.
The bodice is lace, with an embroidered floral pattern that
runs along the sleeves down my arms and across my chest.
There are multiple layers underneath the skirt, and the fabric
feels rough on my legs.

It's my final fitting, so they've made me up more or less
how I will look on the day. My hair has been combed, tamed,
and braided, the braids pinned back in a crown around my
skull. I look elegant, for the first time in…maybe ever. Gone
are my ripped jeans and combat boots.

Enter Rory March—no. Princess Rory.

Why does that still sound so hollow in my ears?

My seamstress pokes me with a pin and quickly apolo-
gizes, but I'm so stunned by my own reflection, I barely even
feel it.

A soft, familiar knock on the door snaps me out of my haze. "Are you decent?"

I turn around and yelp when I see him.

"You can't see me! It's bad luck."

"Only for the groom." Ben hangs in the doorway. He scans me from head to toe and back again. The warmth in his eyes is palpable. "You look amazing, Rory."

I'm suddenly shy. "Thanks." I take the ends and twist my hips a little so the frill spins. "You don't think it's too…?"

"No," he says immediately before I can finish that thought. "It's perfect. It's you."

There's silence between us. There seems to be a lot of silence between us now.

"Miss March!" A housekeeper steps in. "Your mail is here."

"Thanks. You can put them on the bed."

He empties out a whole bag of letters on my bedspread, then leaves me to it.

Ben steps over and runs his finger over a letter. "These are all for you?"

"Yeah." I roll my hair through my fingers absently. "I still have a lot on the bureau, too. I haven't really had time to answer any of them, but I will."

Out of the corner of my eyes, I see Ben picking through the already opened letters on the bureau. He stops when he comes to one and pauses to read through it. "Not all of these are very nice."

I shrug. "I'm a redhead. I'm used to people not being nice to me."

"*Rory.*" Ben's voice is stiff as leather. He holds out a letter. "This is a death threat."

I sigh. "I know… Queen Selena said not to take them too seriously… 'You're not a princess until you get a death threat or ten'—I think those were her actual words."

"How many of those are there?"

Again, I shrug. It's not that I'm trying to be dismissive; I just genuinely don't have an answer for him. Most of the letters are nice, sweet words of encouragement from people who have followed "Hashtag Princess Rory" from the start. Some—the ones I really take time to read—are from people who urge me to take the role seriously. Mothers tell me about their sick children, depressed soldiers beg for more funding for veterans, and families with crippling debt write to me for some solution. I know royalty isn't what it is in the movies; I'm no fairy godmother, and I can't go around leaving money under everyone's pillows. But I still save those letters in a special pile...so that one day, eventually, I can do *something* to help them.

The other letters—the ones spewing hatred, vulgarities, and, yes, sometimes death threats, mostly go ignored by me. It's not that I can't take the heat—I can. But there's also a part of me that's a big fan of the *I'm rubber, you're glue* way of life, and I've had so much to worry about with Roland, Ben, my pregnancy, and the wedding, that I haven't had a second to pay the haters much thought.

Ben sounds concerned, though, and that makes *me* concerned. He's flipping through my letters, but he pauses at one. He lifts it out and says, "Oh."

"What?"

His silence makes my heart pound. He hesitates, as though he's fishing for the right word between his teeth, then finally comes out with it. "I know this sender. The woman who sent you the death threats."

My eyes go wide. "You *know* her?"

Ben has always seemed like such a good judge of character before...why would he make friends with someone who mails out vicious verbal attacks to people she doesn't even know?

Ben looks reluctant, but he says, "There's something you should see."

16

BEN

*H*elmsway Palace does not lack for hidden corridors.

I take Rory into the library. There's a bookshelf that opens up here to reveal a narrow, winding stone staircase, lit with hanging, open-faced bulbs. You take it up, it'll dump you out onto the balcony. It was designed as a way for royalty to duck and run in the event of an assassination attempt, and thankfully, we haven't had to use it for its original purpose.

But we're not going upstairs. We're going down. It ends at a locked stone door. There are only three keys to this door, and I have one of them. I open it up—have to give it a shove; the door has rusted a bit from disuse—and then hold the door for Rory to pass through.

I follow behind and flip on the light. It's a library not entirely unlike the one we passed through, but smaller, dustier, and complete with rows upon rows of marked boxes and filing cabinets. There are a couple tables and chairs to the right that haven't seen a lot of use. A crimson red carpet covers the floor, giving the entire place a *soaked in blood* look.

"What is this place?" Rory asks. She steps around gingerly,

as though afraid a misstep might send the whole place crumbling into a pile of dust.

"The royal archives," I tell her. "Some of it, anyway. Many of our official documents are stored in the Scotland Yard, but we keep the family's personal files here."

I don't spend too much time down here, but I know my way around well enough. I step deeper into the archives until I get to some of the cleaner, more recent boxes. Roland's things. My eyes flit over the labels until I find what I'm looking for. I lift a box off the shelf; it's not heavy, exactly, but it's got weight and I use the handles.

I set it down on a polished table and turn to Rory. "Do you remember when we first met? At the pub?"

A smile crosses her face. "How could I forget? You were the hottest guy there, and you ate me up."

"I seduced you. For Roland. I took you to the palace so we could both share you. You remember when you got here…a guard checked you in. Had you sign a nondisclosure agreement."

Slowly, she nods. "Yeah…the whole night was…a blur. But I remember that."

"And I told you," I explain patiently, "that you weren't the first we'd done with this."

Rory is a smart girl and I can see when it clicks, because her eyes lock on the box with new horror. She points at it. "Is that…?"

I nod. "These are the NDAs—plus background checks— from all the women we've been with."

"*All*," she repeats, the word sounding clunky in her mouth. "I mean, I know I wasn't the first but…how many were there?"

I open the lid. "Do you really want to know?"

I can tell she's sizing up the stack with her eyes. Finally, she shakes her head. "It's in the past." She shrugs. "It doesn't matter. Right?" Then she creeps closer and glances over my shoulder. "Is my file in there?"

"Yes." I take out a manila folder with her name "MARCH, RORY" printed on the tab, and hold it over for her. I know what it says—I read through it a couple billion times when she first came into our lives. She opens it up and sees the basic details mirrored back to her—no criminal record, one brother, two parents, American, went to school, can be seen on her vlog—

She still goes through every page, though. I don't blame her. I would, too.

"This is crazy," she says.

I peel through the folders, then stop at one. "And this," I tell her, "is Imogen Dodds."

I procure a file from the box and drop it on the table.

Rory doesn't pick it up, though. Instead, she keeps her hand at her side, as though she's afraid the folder will bite her. "Imogen…is that the woman who sends me mail? You slept with her?"

"We both did," I say a little too fast—as if that makes it okay.

She shakes her head. "But…if that's true…why come after me?"

I flip open the file. There's a picture of her paperclipped to the documents inside. The photo shows a severe but beautiful woman—black hair in a tight bun, green eyes, small nose, and a sharp mouth. "Could be anything. Jealousy. Resentment."

Rory's hand drops to her stomach, perhaps unconsciously. "Is she dangerous?"

I leave the folders and direct my focus entirely on her. I slip my hands up her arms and tell her, "I'll send someone over with a warning. Demand that she stop sending the letters."

"No, it's…all right…" Rory glances away, tucks her hair

behind her ear, and lets out a light sigh. "I don't want to stir up any drama so close to the wedding, you know?" Then she forces a smile over her lips. "I just won't open them. Problem solved."

"Rory—"

Before I can express any concern, she pushes up on her tiptoes and presses a quick kiss to my lips. "Thank you for showing me this. But I don't want to get the rumor mill going right now. I know your first instinct is always to protect me, but please just…leave this alone for now."

"I understand," I say.

She squints. "You promise?"

"I promise." I make a mental note to do a discreet dig into Dodd's whereabouts, though. Can't hurt and, technically, isn't breaking the promise.

Rory's hands fall and lace with my own. "Let's go back upstairs. It's stuffy in here."

"Couldn't agree more."

I close the box up, put it back on the shelf, and take Rory upstairs. Together, we leave the past in the past.

But I have the nagging feeling it won't stay there long.

17

ROLAND

*O*ur wedding is twenty-four hours away, and the palace is in a panic.

There's a bouquet of flowers in every corner of the palace, it seems, and more keep coming. Our social media accounts are exploding with celebrations across the world— everyone having their own personal royal wedding party, not to mention the thousands of people who flooded London just for this occasion.

Rory and I sit in the throne room with the wedding director. The wedding itself will take place at my family's cathedral, but in the meantime, we're having a rehearsal at the palace. Our director is a calm, practical man, who reminds me a bit of Ben, and he moves us around like pieces on the chessboard until we get it just right.

He's speaking with my mum, now, who is a difficult woman to direct—I should know. I rub my hand over the ornate arm of my chair and it feels Clorox sticky. "It smells like a crime scene in here," I joke, commenting on the lemon-fresh scent that's been sprayed a little too copiously. I glance over at Rory in the plush seat beside mine. She hasn't heard me at all; she's gazing off, distracted, her emerald eyes distant and unfocused.

"Earth to Rory," I say, and she blinks back at me.

"Sorry...I'm just...elsewhere."

"Take me there. Seems like a wonderful place if it's hogging all your attention."

"The opposite." Her lips are pressed into thin, thoughtful lines. "Can I ask you a question?"

"Certainly."

"Why me?"

I blink. "How do you mean?"

"I mean...out of all the women you and Ben have been with...why me? Was I just...the only one who forced myself into your life?"

"No. Rory." I put my hand over hers. "You're special. I knew that from the first moment I saw you. There was something different about you."

"Different like...American?"

I shake my head. "No. But—yes. That is very sexy. It's not the thing that drew me to you. It was your otter."

Now, a smile slowly climbs her face. "My otter?"

"Yes. You carried that stuffed animal with you on your trips so part of your brother was always with you. When you told me that story...it opened up my heart. The depth of your compassion and love for your brother changed something in me. All my life, I've been bound to rules and traditions. People loved me because I was the queen's son. They respected me because of *what* I was...not *who* I was. You looked at me and...you saw straight through me. You saw the man underneath the crown."

"And at that moment," Rory presses, "love and compassion were more important than tradition. Right?"

I know what she's doing. She's goading me, trying to get me to say that traditions—like this wedding—aren't important. I set my jaw and then say, "At that moment. Yes. But things are more complicated now."

"Why? Because I'm—?" She stops herself from saying it all the way. There are people in the room with us, after all, my mom nearly in earshot, and we've agreed not to tell anyone about her pregnancy until after the wedding. So instead, she edits herself with "Because I'm baking a cake?"

I pull my lips in. "Partly," I say. "It changes things."

"It doesn't *have* to."

I let out a sharp, frustrated breath. I'm trying to keep my temper—a real challenge for me, by the way. Ben is much better at this part. Reining in his emotions and having a normal, adult conversation.

I'm not. I know she sees it all on my face—she's being, frankly, immature about this, and that's coming from *me*. And I know now is not the time or place to bring this up, but I'm irritated and I make bad decisions when my emotions get the best of me, so I just spit it out. "Have you thought about getting the test?"

She scrunches her eyebrows. "What test?"

"You know." I lift my eyebrows knowingly. "To see whose…*cake*…it is."

Her jaw squares off. "No. And I'm not going to."

That answer catches me off guard. "Why not?"

"Because it doesn't matter to me."

"Maybe it doesn't make a difference to you—" We're getting heated; my voice is raising, and I know I should stop but I can't—she calls me her lion for a reason, and when I get angry, I roar. "—but it makes a damn good deal of a difference to the British people."

"I didn't *ask* to be a princess!" Rory snaps. And now *everyone* is looking at us because she's on her feet, shouting at me. "I fell in love with you *despite* your crown, Roland, not because of it. You of all people should know that!"

She's wild now, her hair like fire bursting from her head.

Her words leave a stone in my throat, but I try to calm her with her name. "Rory…"

"I think I've had enough of this. *All* of this!" She rips her veil from her head and tosses it on the table. "If you want a princess so much, you can marry your damn self."

With that, she storms out of the room. I can feel everyone's eyes on me, and my skin feels as though it's grown spikes.

I spent so many of my days growing up praying for the day that I could escape the walls of this palace, the pressure and the paranoia that came with it. Now, I want nothing more than to go to my room, close the door, and hole away.

But everyone in this room is looking at me. *Me*. For guidance. And this prince won't hide.

I paint on a smile and turn to our pastry chef. "Miss Thompson, would you mind stepping in for Rory?"

She can't hide the smile that splits across her face. "It'd be an honor, Your Highness," she replies with a curtsy.

I've made Miss Thompson's day, but I've ruined Rory's. One for one, I suppose.

"Once more!" I announce to everyone, taking control of the scene. "So everyone can learn their cues. Thank you."

Immediately, people scurry to their places. I can take control of the room with ease…but I'm not arrogant enough to think that I can control Rory.

Nor do I want to. My kitten will come to me on her own terms…or not at all.

And all I can do is wait at the altar and pray.

18

BEN

*M*ost days, I love my job. Today isn't one of those days.

Mapping a security plan for the wedding is a bloody nightmare. All the cameras have been checked and double-checked so there aren't any blind spots. We've tripled our team of guards, which means a whole new round of background checks, showing them around the estate, making sure there's one stationed every few meters. It's damn near midnight and I'm still playing whack-a-mole with my problems, trying to knock one down before the next pops up.

I've got a crick in my neck from hunching over my computer at my desk, and I almost don't notice Rory until the patter of slippers on hardwood catches my attention. She's leaning in the doorway, wearing nothing but a long band T-shirt—her sleepwear of choice.

"Hi," she says. "Am I interrupting?"

"Not a bad thing." I roll my chair back a little, disconnecting myself from my world and focusing entirely on Rory. "Is everything all right?"

"Can't sleep." She shrugs. "I think it's just jitters about tomorrow."

We've been using words like that lately—vague intonations of the thing instead of saying the thing itself. *Marriage, wedding*—it's like she's banned those words from her vocabulary around me. This past week in particular, we've started dancing around subjects, using child gloves with each other, and removing words completely from sentences, leaving long, awkward, yawning pauses instead. I'm not sure if this is a phase or simply how it's going to be from now on.

"Where's Roland?" I ask.

She shrugs again. "I guess he's jittery, too."

I can picture Roland—he's either in the drawing room, tickling the ivory keys of the grand piano, or in the game room, playing a solo game of darts. His two go-to activities to clear his head.

Rory draws her foot in a semicircle across the floor, shifting her weight. "If you're…not too busy," she ventures hesitantly. "Can we watch *Friends*?"

Friends. Rory's television comfort food.

I am busy. But not too busy for her. I close my laptop. "I'll get the ice cream."

* * *

THERE AREN'T any name brands in the palace, just tubs of premade homemade ice cream. I make myself a small bowl of pistachio nut, and Rory scoops huge chunks of cookie dough into her bowl. There are plenty of huge, wide-screen televisions to choose from, but most of the entertainment rooms are occupied by the palace's plethora of guests, maids, and bodyguards, so we go into the one room that isn't packed— the library. Only it's too bright in here for a proper cinematic setting—the old, gold-hue lamps that hang above don't exactly dim—so we build a small movie-watching tent out of chairs, blankets, and throw pillows. Rory props her computer up on a pillow on the floor, plugs in her external hard drive, and queues up her favorite season of *Friends* (season five). Once it's all set, she scrambles back to cuddle up beside me, our backs against the couch. I hand her the bowl of ice cream, she thanks me, and then hits Play with her big toe.

We've seen these episodes a thousand times, so I don't have to concern myself so much with following the plot. Instead, I shift my attention to Rory. She's leaning against me, swirling her spoon around her ice cream. The bags under her eyes are deep. She's exhausted but can't sleep.

I want her to open up, but I don't want to pry it out of her. So I reach my spoon over and steal a chunk of cookie dough from her bowl.

"Hey!" she laughs. "Thief!"

"Not thief. Bodyguard tax."

That makes her laugh again. I love that sound. Her laugh turns into a groan, and she drops her head against my shoulder. "I missed this."

"Missed what?"

"*This*. Just…being normal."

"You're normal?"

"You know what I mean," Rory sighs. "Not…all *princessy*."

"Mm."

Rory's spoon clinks against her bowl a couple of times before she comes out with "I don't know how Roland does it. The…royal hoopla of it all. It's enough to make someone crazy."

"To be fair…he's had twenty-seven years of training." I've eaten my fill, so I set my bowl aside and wrap my arm around her shoulders. She snuggles in a little tighter, and I continue. "But Roland has always only been Roland. He doesn't follow rules, he makes them. And he expects no more or less from you."

She hesitates at that. "Yeah. I guess."

"Hey." I take her chin in my fingers and tilt her head so

her gaze meets mine. "He loves you. More than anything. And he'd never force you to do something you don't want. If you're having second thoughts about this wedding…"

"No," Rory says quickly—too quickly, maybe. "I'm not. It's…just the baby." She shrugs, brushing it off. "Hormones. I'll be fine in the morning."

She's lying, but I can tell she doesn't want to be pushed. So I don't push it. Instead, I rest my hand over her shoulder and rub my thumb into the bare skin there until she settles against me.

We refocus our attention on the show. We're halfway through the next episode when I hear footsteps approach. A shadow grows larger against our tent, and then the side of the blanket lifts. Roland pokes his head underneath, his blond hair flattening against the top of the tent as he looks around. "Nice setup you've got here."

"We're in hiding," I explain.

"Good idea. Room for one more?" he asks.

I glance to Rory. She nods. "Always room for one more," she says.

I shift to make space for him. Roland climbs in and flops down on the other side of Rory. He's still dressed in his white button-up and nice trousers, but he's untucked his shirt and undone the top buttons. I prefer the messy version of him.

"Rory," he says, his voice suddenly serious. "About earlier…I'm sorry, I shouldn't have—"

"No, I'm sorry," she interrupts. "We were both stressed." She holds up her bowl of ice cream. "Peace treaty?"

He lets out a soft chuckle and takes the bowl. "Look at you. You'll be negotiating world peace in no time."

"I'm a natural," she says.

They kiss. I hear that familiar, soft sigh of Rory's. Something about it makes me ache, and not in a good way.

"Let's go to bed," Rory says. But before she can turn to me, I shift to my feet, crouching so I don't disrupt the tent.

"I'm going to clean up." I grab the empty ice cream bowls. "I'll meet you there."

I slip out before either of them can protest. I need a minute. I can't say what it is exactly, but suddenly I feel like it's two years ago, before Rory, back when I was Roland's bodyguard and *only* that. Bottled up with pining for something I can't have.

I take the bowls to the kitchen, pick a cigarette out from my pack, and wait until the feelings subside.

19

RORY

*I*t's here.

My wedding day. A royal wedding. I'm in Roland's bedroom, while women flutter and flock around me, adjusting my dress, my hair, and my makeup. On the hanging TV, I can see a full crowd pressed against the iron gates. The *Normals*, as Queen Selena calls them. The high-society people are *inside* the gates. The palace is bustling with people. Outside the window, I can see the garden flush with lush flowers. There are tables set up, a live band, and an ice sculpture. They've got a feast spread out on the tables as a pre-wedding cocktail party for society elites, dukes, and duchesses. I'm supposed to make my way down there, enter-tain them for five minutes before I'm swept away into the crowd of rabid royal wedding fans.

But I can't bring my legs to take me in that direction. Dukes and lords are things in fairy tales. This isn't the life I'm used to. My thoughts are spinning a mile a minute, and only half of them make sense. This is supposed to be the happiest day of my life.

So why can't I catch my breath?

It might have something to do with the designer tightening my bust within an inch of my life. I gasp as she cinches the laces, and my hand goes to my stomach.

"That's enough, thank you," I tell her quickly. I don't need this baby flying out of me all pressure-cooked.

"We've got to head out in fifteen, Mrs. March," Sam calls out from the doorway.

"Miss March," I correct. "Not missus. Not yet."

I'm start to sweat. I feel it start to drip from my scalp and down my face. I try to dab it away, knowing how hard the artist has worked on my makeup.

Maybe it would help if my parents were here. But Oscar can't travel right now, so they stayed with him. I think about calling them for a moment; maybe it would calm me to see their faces. Hear his voice. Oscar always calms me.

But…it's not them I want. Not really.

It's *Ben*.

Each thought swirls back to him. And when I'm in this state—hands shaking, heart hammering in my chest…*I need Ben*. He's the only person in the world who can calm me right now. I need him to wrap his hand around my throat, look me in the eyes, and tell me in that calm, deep voice of his that I've got this and everything is going to be okay.

I need *him*.

I have tunnel vision, and I don't see Sam rush to me until she's beside me. I reach out and clutch her arm. "You okay, Miss March?" she asks.

"I need Ben," I say. My throat is tight, and my voice comes out nearly as a whisper.

"Okay, we'll call him—"

"No." I squeeze her arm. I know I'm clinging too tightly, but I can't relax my hold. My heart feels like it's going to beat right out of my chest. "Go get him. *Now*. I'm not…I *can't*—"

"Okay," she says, and this time she smiles placatingly. "Don't worry about it, okay? I'll be *right* back."

"Thank you," I say. My throat closes again, and my

whole body feels like it's vibrating. I think I hear Sam talking to one of the attendant, telling her to keep an eye on me before my bodyguard rushes off. I close my eyes, tilt my head back, and put my hand around my throat. It's not Ben, but maybe it'll help. I know I must look insane—crazy American girl self-asphyxiating—which must be why one of the girls comes over and puts her hands on me.

"Come on, dear," she says. "Let's get your makeup touched up, yeah?"

"Okay," I say, but my voice sounds hollow in my own ears. I don't want to sit for makeup, I don't want them to pull at my hair anymore and turn me into someone I'm not. I want Ben to wrap his hand around my throat; I want Roland to tell me we're doing the right thing.

One of the maids comes in with a bottle of champagne, and everyone flocks to it like seagulls to french fries—*what a good idea!* And *just what we need, pop it open, then.*

While everyone is distracted, it occurs to me that this is my chance.

I know the palace like the back of my hand and—more than that—I know all of the little sneaky passages, intended to use for royalty in the event of an attack. But I'm *almost* royalty today, so while everyone flocks to the bubbles, I press my fingertips into a fake panel in the wall and feel it give under my touch, revealing a hidden staircase. I tuck into the short opening, pull my dress in with me, and quietly close the panel behind me.

It's quieter here at the top of an old, spiral staircase, illuminated by hazy open bulbs. My vision is still blurry, my heart beating way too quickly in my chest. This staircase will drop me out the back, and right now, the breath of fresh air seems necessary. Like a child, I clutch the walls and fumble downstairs until I find the exit. It's glaringly bright out here, and I blink against the overbearing sun. I nearly trip over a pot of flowers that's not normally there—and this is *wrong*, all of this is wrong.

A hand moves to my shoulder to break my fall. *Ben*, the hopeful part of my brain thinks. But this man's hands are soft, his fingers too thin, and his voice too smooth when he speaks. "This way, miss," he says.

"No, I can't go," I protest. My eyes are still adjusting to the light, my panic attack making my vision into slits, and all I see of this man is a lanky form and black hat. I try to pull away, but his hand encircles my wrist like cuffs. "I need to see Ben."

"Right you are," he says calmly—how is everyone so calm? "He's right this way, miss."

Thank God, I think. Finally, someone who will take me to Ben. Ben, who will instantly know what's wrong, who won't ask questions, won't judge me; he'll just take me in his strong arms, kiss me, and wrap his hands around my throat until the pounding in my veins slows and all the pins and needles flush out of my blood.

Relief feels close, so close now. I'm stumbling across the walkway, out the back, and this is a bit strange, because I know these steps. We're walking *away* from the palace, not toward it. Why would Ben have left?

"Are you sure Ben's this way?" I ask.

I see the back of his peacoat as the strange man drags me along.

"Yes, Miss Rory," he says.

But this feels *wrong*, like in a bad dream when you know something is altered but it's impossible to put your finger on it. I don't see Ben ahead—instead, I see a black car. Waiting. On the side of the road.

My feet come to a stop. "Who did you say you are, again?" I ask.

"I didn't, miss," he responds. But there's a cruel twist in

his mouth that sends a spike of fresh terror through my heart.

I think about the palace—everyone hustling, preparing for the wedding. Roland. In his beautiful suit, standing at the altar for me.

"I need to go back," I say. "Roland is waiting for me." I yank my hand away, but his grip tightens. He turns on me, and suddenly all the warmth has left his face.

"You aren't going anywhere, I'm afraid."

He draws something from his pocket—a blue handker-chief—and suddenly he catches the back of my head and covers my mouth with the blue square. I try to scream, but my voice is muffled by his palm and the fabric. There's a terrible, acidic chemical smell in the handkerchief. I try to struggle, try to pull away, but my limbs feel heavy now and warm. I can't keep my eyes open, and the last thing I see is the sky as I feel myself falling into the arms of this stranger.

"It's all right, princess," he growls, his hot breath hitting my face. "I've got you now."

20

BEN

*A*s the ceremony unfolds outside, I remain inside. In my lair.

It's quiet here, nothing but the familiar buzz and whir of electronics. My earpiece crackles for a while with cues, guest list inquiries, and call times. Someone needs to be down here. Keep an eye on things.

But I don't have to be sober while doing it.

It's not much, but I've brought a little flask down here with me, and every now and then, I take a nip off it.

I'm not bitter. I'm not allowed to be bitter. This was all my bloody idea, after all.

And as soon as they say their *I dos* and tie the knot, I'm going to be happy for them. I'm going to smile, kiss them, and wish them the best of luck. I'm going to be there for them—like I always have and always will.

But we have almost an hour until that bit, and so until then, I'm going to take a little time to be selfish about the whole thing.

One hour. That's all I've allotted myself. Be selfish. Be indulgent. Wallow. And then move on.

I'm a beer bloke, not a whisky bloke, but after a couple

swallows, it stops tasting so sharp and I'm able to enjoy it. I lean back in my chair and scan the screens in front of me. The palace that I've watched over tirelessly for seven years looks completely different today. There are streamers out front. Huge floral arrangements stuffed with Alice in Wonderland flowers—crying calla lilies and blue and violet larkspurs. Maids hustle about, all their uniforms washed and pressed.

Soon, Rory will walk out in her stunning, white wedding gown. She'll look beautiful. Roland will, too, in his dark suit. He'll be wearing the ring his father gave him. His suit jacket will have his family crest on his lapel. They'll make a breathtaking couple, and all of England will fawn over them.

I remove the earpiece, turning it off for a moment and setting it down on the desk.

Sam and Benjamin have this covered. They don't need me. No one needs me—not right now, anyway.

I'm in a tux, and the temperature in the room must be off, because right now the suit feels stifling. I pop open a couple of the top buttons so I can breathe.

My chair fits to my form when I slouch back in it. "Cheers to the happy couple," I murmur, raising my flask once toward the screens before tilting it against my lips.

I close my eyes. I relish the cold, empty relief of silence.

But luck is not on my side today, because as soon as I start to relax, my thigh buzzes. I lift my cell and my jaw clenches when I see the caller ID. *This better be important.*

"What?" I ask when I answer the call.

"Er, sorry to be a bother, boss," Benjamin stammers. "I was just wondering—is Miss March with you?"

"No. Why would she be with me?"

"It's just…well, she was asking about you."

She was asking about me. My heart hiccups on the beat inside my chest. My kitten still needs me. "Tell her I'll be right there," I say, and almost hang up the phone when he interrupts me.

"Well, that the *problem*, boss. No one can seem to find her, exactly."

My blood goes cold. "I'm on my way."

21

ROLAND

"*To* have and to hold…I take you…I *take* you…"

I pace back and forth in the tight confines of my room. When pacing doesn't do it, I vibrate my lips together in little "brrrrip!" sounds. And I rehearse an improv phrase or two: "Red leather, yellow leather, red leather, yellow leather—don't you, can't you, want you, won't you—"

Great actors always warm up before a show, so I'm trying to follow in their footsteps. Today needs to be perfect. Not for England, not for the royal family, hell, not even for my mum.

It needs to be perfect for *Rory*. She deserves that. She deserves a perfect, flawless wedding.

So I practice. "Red leather, yellow—"

The door clicks and swings open. When I see the man on the other side, relief sweeps through me like a warm summer breeze. "Ben," I say. "It's damn good to see you, mate."

But he doesn't look quite as pleased to see me. Instead, his lips pull together in a thin line, his thick eyebrows draw together, and his jaw tightens.

We've always been able to speak without words, and his face is screaming at me.

I feel my smile fall. "What's wrong?"

His eyes drop to the floor. He's gathering the courage to talk to me. Finally, he seems to have it, because his searing dark eyes meet mine and don't let go with time. "It's Rory. She's gone."

And just like that, the floor falls out from under me.

A voice that sounds terribly much like my mum murmurs in my ear, *You're not enough, and you never will be.*

"She…ran?" I ask.

"No," Ben says, and before I have time to feel relief, he adds, "She was kidnapped."

What was once self-loathing turns into pure, abject fear.

My breath has left my body, but then I steel my nerves. "Tell me everything."

2 2

RORY

I'm blindfolded.

His lips taste my throat, all the way up to my ear. "We're going to play a game," Ben murmurs, his breath warm on my face.

I'm strapped to the bed—I can feel the rope bite into my wrists. I like the way the rope feels on my wrists, and being immobilized, at their mercy...it makes my breath catch and my heart beat a little faster.

"Okay..." I can't stop grinning. "I'm listening."

"Spread your legs," Ben says, so I do. I'm completely naked, and showing myself to them like this...I feel both vulnerable and incredibly hot.

"Now"—Ben's voice guides me through it—"one of us is going to lick you. And you have to guess who it is."

I bite my bottom lip. I'm trying not to laugh through this —but I'm excited! "Okay..." I say.

"And if you guess wrong," Ben says, his voice suddenly hard, "there will be punishment."

I'm not afraid of punishment—my men would never do anything I don't like. Instead, I'm achingly curious. But I want to be a good girl for them, so I nod and say, "Okay."

"Okay?"

"Yes, boss."

"Good, kitten."

As if by way of reward, I feel a tongue swirl between my legs. A gasp gets stuck in my throat, surprise rippling through me along with a bolt of pleasure. The tongue is warm, savoring, taking its time licking every inch of me.

"Roland," I say breathlessly.

"You're right. Good work, kitten." That's Roland's voice—though I wish he'd stop talking and keep doing what he was doing. Instead, he pulls back, and I feel wet and achy between my legs.

There's a pause before sensation comes back. This tongue intrudes. It parts my slippery lips and presses deep inside of me, tasting the most intimate parts of me.

I groan and lift my hips toward his lips. When Ben's beard scratches in a lovely way against my inner thighs, I manage to get out, "Ben."

It stops again. The start-and-stop teasing with their tongues is driving me insane. I don't want it to stop, ever, but I want to play their game. So when I feel it on me again, teasing my swollen little nub, I gasp, "Roland…"

Suddenly, the tongue vanishes and, instead, I feel a sharp slap between my legs. I yelp in surprise, and my body goes rigid. It doesn't hurt, exactly, but it startles me and sends a tingling sensation all over me. My nether lips, which were already plump, now feel so swollen and achy.

"Wrong," Ben says. "I told you that you would be punished."

"Yes, boss," I murmur, delirious with pleasure.

"What do you say?"

"Thank you for punishing me."

"Let's try that again." I feel wet, slippery warmth between my legs, so much more intense now on my raw sex, and my thoughts scatter. They go back and forth, back and forth, one licking, then the other, and I keep guessing, but it's getting harder. More than that—I start guessing the wrong name on purpose. I love the slaps to my sex as much as I love the kisses, and the mixture of both makes my head spin and sends me spiraling.

My sex clenches; I'm swollen, achy, and I've drenched these sheets—in sweat, their saliva, and my own desperate arousal. Each lash of their tongues sends a spike of hot pleasure through me until I don't think I can take any more. Someone—Roland? Ben?—has been between my legs for a long time now, licking, nibbling, and sucking all my most sensitive bits, until it stops and Roland asks, "Well?"

"Uhm…" I bite my lip. "I don't…know. Just…please."

"Please what?"

"Please…slap it again." My hips push forward, begging, and my throat is so tight, I feel like I might cry. "I need it."

He does. This time, when his hand smacks me between the legs, everything in me explodes. I shout as my orgasm rips through me without warning, breaking over his palm. Ben gives my sex quicker little taps, letting me ride it out, and I quiver and jerk against the binds. "Please," I whimper. "Please, please, please…"

"Oh, quit begging, won't you? It's positively *droll*."

The voice startles me. That's not Ben. That's not Roland. It's not even a *man*. It's a woman. My warm, lovely memory scatters and I'm dropped back into the cold real world. I catch my breath and immediately try to reorient myself. It's still dark when I open my eyes—something is blocking my vision—but when I try to reach up to remove it, I find my hands bound behind my back. I'm not in bed…and I am wearing clothes, a small blessing. But even as my memory fades, the bits that have remained are jarring: the bind around my wrists is tighter than Ben would ever make it, and the itchy ropes bites into my skin. I'm sitting on the floor, and there's a bar behind me, pressed against my spine, but that's all I can discern. The room smells like sweat and rubber, like a gym.

Where am I? And who is she? I can't hear for the pounding in my ears. My head is still hazy. The last thing I remember is getting ready for my wedding... I was getting ready, and I needed *Ben*. And then—there was a man. Fear shudders through me when I remember how he covered my mouth, the harsh, chemical smell of the cloth.

My heart tumbles around in my chest. But whatever this is...I know one thing for sure. I can't let them see how terrified I am. I swallow hard, tilt my chin in the direction of the woman's voice, and ask, "Where am I?"

"Arthur!" The woman's voice comes out as a screech, and I jump in place. "She's awake!"

Footsteps clomp into the room and draw closer. Suddenly, a pair of hands grips me and yanks me closer. I yelp when he removes my blindfold roughly.

It's the man who drugged me. My bones turn to ice. Any trace of fake warmth that he'd put on at the wedding is gone now. He's still dressed in a smart button-up, but his face looks hard and mean, a boxy jaw unkempt with black stubble. He has a water bottle in one hand, and he grabs my chin and forces my head up.

"Drink," he says, shoving the water bottle at my mouth.

I try to yank away—I've been drugged once already, and I don't want to be drugged again. I throw my body backward, but he catches me by the hair and dumps the water over my mouth. I choke and gag as it splashes over me, swallowing some of it, until finally he pushes me away and takes the water bottle with him.

"And they call *her* princess," the woman's voice scoffs. I turn in the direction of the noise. I can finally see my surroundings, but none of this makes sense. I'm sitting on hardwood floor and surrounded by a wall of mirrors, like I'm in a fun house. No. Not a fun house. A dance studio.

There's a horizonal bar along the wall across from me, and another bar behind me—it's what I've been tied to. Thick bunches of fabric hang like hammocks from the ceiling. In the corner of the room is a pile of mats and an open doorway to an assortment of props, Hula-Hoops, and ropes.

The bizarre surroundings make me dizzy, that feeling I get when I'm aboard a plane that's swooped on descent. My vision keeps doubling, and I'm trying to keep it all in one place. There's a woman sitting on a stool across from me, but my pupils vibrate and she turns into two women, then one again. Finally, her form crystalizes. She has an athlete's figure, with a boyish frame, square hips, and long, midnight-black hair that falls down her shoulders.

When she looks at me, her lips curl in a sneer and I can't figure out why. I don't *know* this woman. "Who are you?" I ask. And then: "What do you want from me?"

"Oh, dear," she sighs. She steps off the stool with a dancer's elegance, toes pointing and then flattening out on the polished floor underneath. When she walks, however, it's with a small but noticeable limp. She crouches down in front of me and cups my face in her hand, her thumb rubbing hard over my cheek like an aggressively affectionate grandmother. "I don't want anything from *you*. It's the prince I want, obviously. Though now that I see you…I can't for the life of me figure out why they chose *you*. A frightened little deer, aren't you?"

She's not wrong. I am frightened. And she said *they*, not *he*, which means…she knows Roland, Ben, and I are a package deal. Right? But that still hasn't answered the *why* of this.

I don't want to show any more fear than I already have. My years spent traveling solo taught me that the more vulnerable and out of place you look, the more likely you are to get pickpocketed, or worse. So I seal my lips together.

"This isn't the way to do it. To get what you want. When Roland finds me—"

"Silly girl," she hisses, her tone venomous. "You don't know a bloody thing about him."

She extracts herself from me, and I'm glad for that—the sharpness in her eyes is lethal. She paces away from me instead and rakes her fingers through her hair. In the mirror, I can see the deep contemplation on her face. The man who dragged me here—the scary, bulldoggish one—sits on a stool near the door, watching her like a loyal pet waiting on his master's next command.

It strikes me then. Through the haze and the blurriness in my head. A sudden realization: "You're Imogen. The woman who sent me the letters."

She whips around suddenly, her eyes fixing on me, wide with surprise. And then, slowly, a fox-like smile crawls over her face. "Clever girl," she says and turns her gaze to the man. "Not as dumb as she looks, is she?"

She tilts her head toward the man and then says, "I'm bored of it. Drug her again."

"You sure about that?" he says. "I already gave her quite a bit—"

"Do I look like I bloody care?" she snaps.

He stands. He grabs two things from the small folding table beside him—the handkerchief and a small vial of clear liquid—and my adrenaline spikes. He approaches me, lumbering like a golem, and pours the vial into the handkerchief. "Please, don't," I beg, no longer able to hide the panic in my voice. "I won't tell anyone—I'll stop talking…please…"

But he doesn't slow down, he doesn't stop; his feet keep toward me at the same excruciating pace, until finally, when he extends his hand to press the cloth to my face, I shout:

"I'm pregnant!"

He stops. Surprise flickers through his big, dull eyes. He glances back at Imogen, who raises her eyebrows. "Well?"

When he hesitates, she scoffs and rolls her eyes. "Bloody useless you are, brother."

Her bare feet cross the distance soundlessly. She snatches the handkerchief from his hand, gets down on her knees, and says with cloying sweetness, "If it was meant to be, this won't hurt but a pinch."

Then the blue cloth covers my face and my world goes black again.

23

BEN

*T*he wedding is on hold.

Queen Selena and her entourage are taking care of it. I'm not sure what excuse they've came up with—and, frankly, I don't care.

The wedding is no longer my priority. Rory's safety is.

I'm in my office with Roland at my side, flanked by our security's team leaders, and we're all fixed on my computer monitor.

I've managed to pull up footage I found earlier of the south gate. There's no sound to it, but we can see Rory exit through one of the back doors. Hard to miss her in her big, flowing wedding dress. She's stumbling, dazed—she looks drunk, but I know better. She's in a panic attack haze. I've seen it plenty of times before. Panic attacks are, unfortunately, something that Rory suffers from with regularity. We had a system, the two of us, when she gets like that.

She panics, I put my hands on her throat and squeeze, and slowly, she'll start to calm down.

The thought of her floundering, looking for me…it sends a shard of glass through my heart.

But I can't think like that right now. Because the video continues.

A man comes up to her. He takes her arm and guides her for a bit. No one else on the lawn seems to think anything of it—he looks like he belongs. The camera doesn't follow them, but we can see her legs slump and go weak. She falls into his arms, and he carries her into a waiting car, which takes off.

"We didn't get the license plate," Sam says, and she sounds mournful about it. "But…" She taps the keyboard and rewinds the video, pausing it where we can get a view of Rory's captor's face.

"That's the reporter from on Christmas Eve," I say. "Gideon Calder."

"Yes and no," Sam says. "He *is* the man who stalked you at your parents' house, boss…but his name isn't Gideon Calder. The press pass was a fake. So we dug in. His real name is Arthur Dodds."

"Arthur Dodds," Roland echoes. His palm is pressed to my desk as he hunches over the monitor, but he looks at me now. "Why does that name sound familiar?"

To say it out loud feels like tinfoil between my teeth. *How could I be so blind that I didn't see this coming?* "Imogen Dodds," I growl. "She's been…writing Rory. Sending threatening letters."

"We looked up Arthur Dodds and Imogen Dodds," Sam explains. "Checked their addresses, but no one's seen them for days."

"Imogen…" Roland rolls the name around his tongue, and then his eyebrows furrow. "You don't mean…?" His gaze flickers around the room briefly, awkward in front of these people, so instead he leans closer, drops his voice, and murmurs, "*That* Imogen. The one we took to bed."

I blink. "You remember her?" I don't know why that surprises me. Perhaps because I nearly didn't remember. I barely remember any of the women that came before Rory. Because I never truly *wanted* those women.

I wanted *him*.

The man who looks at me now with a sharp glare, as though insulted by the suggestion that his memory might be anything less than perfect. "Of course I do. You're forgetting that this palace was my entire world back then. As were the people that moved in and out of it." He sighs and then closes his eyes, before reciting, "Imogen Dodds, sales representative by day, ballerina by passion. From London. Said she would've had a career of dancing, too, if it wasn't for her bum leg. Terrible tragic story."

I don't have time to sympathize with the devil. "Anything else?"

If he can remember something useful…maybe we can find Imogen before she hurts Rory. And the baby.

Roland shakes his head, eyes falling back on the monitor. "I remember she left welts down my back the next morning. Big ones. Like a bloody cougar."

So she's comfortable with violence. That makes my stomach churn. I try not to think about her leaving welts on Rory. "Anything that might be of some *use* to us," I press. "Anything that might tell us where she's taken Rory?"

Roland stares at the monitor, but his gaze is lost. At first, I wonder if he's even heard me. Then after a long, contemplative moment, he finally murmurs without turning his head, "She looks beautiful in that dress, doesn't she?"

That catches me off guard. I don't know what to say.

Then Roland's head drops, his hair falling around his face, hiding it. "Three Swans," he says.

"What?"

"Three Swans." He rakes his hair back and then looks at me. Those blue eyes are shining, wet. "That was the name of Imogen's ballet studio."

I can breathe again. We have a name. And a destination. It's not Rory—but it's a *start*.

"Let's go."

Roland looks so wilted right now, so devastated, and I want to comfort him—I do—but I don't have time or the emotional space for this. I have a mission, and I have to *go*. I have to find Rory. I have to save our baby. I half expect him to put up a fight, but he doesn't. He sniffs instead, pulls himself together, and straightens up. "Benjamin and Sam," he says, motioning them. "You come with us. Everyone else, keep things steady here."

I let out a small breath of relief. Roland's going to be my partner in this—not another body I have to worry about. He grabs my shoulder, gives a squeeze, and his eyes are vibrant when they meet mine. "Come on," he says, "Let's go get our girl."

24

RORY

*W*hen I blink my eyes open, I see little feet kicking in the air. Back and forth, they swish-swish-swish, two little white sneakers. The shoelaces are undone on his left shoe, and they dangle down like snakes.

My gaze travels upward. A little boy sits on a stool, drawing at a round table. He has a full head of curly, blond hair, which bounces as he doodles.

Something else is different. To my left, a video camera stands on a tripod. The camera is plugged into to a laptop on a table behind it. It's aimed at the table. It looks as though it's set to film something, but I'm not sure *what*.

"Mummy," the boy says when he sees me. "The woman woke up."

Mummy. The word sends a shot of panic through me. My hand jolts down and cups my stomach. *I can move my arms.* They're no long tied behind my back, but I'm no less trapped. I'm still stuck in the room of mirrors.

And my baby. The little bump is still there. I'm not sure— can't be sure—but I feel it, the life still burning brightly inside of me, like a firefly bouncing around a mason jar. My anxiety sizzles and dies, collecting into a dull throb in my forehead.

Imogen is sitting on the other side of the table from the small boy. She watches me warily, the way a rattlesnake might a mongoose. "Don't worry about her, love," she coos. "She's not feeling very well."

She's not wrong about that—I feel like crap. It's like the worst hangover of my life, multiplied by ten. The floor feels cold against my cheek. I've drooled and my face feels wet when I peel myself up to a sitting position.

I'm still in my ridiculously poofy wedding dress, and the mesh feels like razor blades against my legs. Everything is *uncomfortable*. I brace my palm against the floor and feel a wave of nausea roll over me. A dry heave claws out of my throat—I haven't had anything to eat, I have nothing in my stomach—and I clutch my little baby bump tighter.

A ringing explodes in my ears, but I can hear the fuzzy voice of Imogen, and it sounds like she's telling someone to *stay there*. But out of the corner of my eyes, I see the swinging feet fall to the floor. The boy approaches me and—this close —I can get a good look at him. He can't be older than four, but he's dressed like an adult, in little-person slacks and a shirt that's buttoned all the way up to his neck.

He lifts a water bottle and holds it up for me. "Excuse me, miss. Are you thirsty?"

He's so polite that I have to press my lips in a warm smile. I reach out to take the bottle. "Thank you, sweetheart."

Whatever this is—he's an innocent here. My hands shake when I lift the bottle to my lips and take little, tiny sips.

"What's your name?" I ask him. Imogen isn't going to hurt me as long as her little boy is around—I can tell that much. The longer I can draw this out, maybe, the longer I can prolong whatever wickedness she has up her sleeve.

He tugs at his shirt nervously. "Um...Nathan," he says.

Those dark eyes look at me, though, unwavering when he asks, "What's yours?"

"Rory."

"It's nice to meet you," he recites, and then adds, "I like your dress."

The breath of the laugh that leaves my chest is genuine, despite this twisted situation. "Thank you," I say. "I'm getting married."

"Oh." Those little wheels behind his curious eyes working. "Where's your husband?"

"*Little prince*," Imogen hisses. "Your shoes."

"Sorry," he says and hurriedly crouches down. He struggles with his shoelaces, but I see the intensity in his furrowed brow—the boy is *trying* so hard.

"Do you want me to help?" I ask.

"*No*. For Christ's sake, come here," Imogen sighs. He bows his head guiltily and shuffles over to his mother. She lifts him into her lap and reaches over to tie his undone shoelaces.

I take the moment to assess my situation. *What would Ben do?* Ben, my former military boyfriend, would look for exits. As far as I can tell, there's only one—a door that's closed. And I'd have to charge past Imogen to do it. Which, maybe, I could…if my legs didn't feel like they had a block of concrete attached to them. I don't see Imogen's brother anywhere, though, so that's a good sign—right? If nothing else, he creeps me out, and it's nice to have one less thing to deal with.

Now that I've figured out the exits, there's the next thing —a weapon. The ropes that once held my wrists are unbound in a bunch behind me. In a pinch, I could grab it, maybe, and use it to choke her before I make my exit…

But I'm *not* a soldier. I've never choked anyone before. I don't know if I'm capable of it…especially with a kid caught in the middle.

My best bet? Wait this out. Draw it out. *My men are*

coming for me. I know they are. Until then, I just have to buy a little time.

As if she can hear my thoughts, Imogen's eyes lock on me. And they narrow. "He's a beautiful boy, isn't he?" she asks. Her voice is light and airy, but there's a vicious, serpentine undertone to her words. She slips her fingers through her boy's thick hair. "He takes after me, obviously. But you can see Roland in him, can't you? The hair. The eyes."

I'm not going to choke her out, maybe, but I also don't have to play her sick games. So I press my lips into a tight smile and correct her. "Roland's eyes are blue. So."

Her lips pull back in a snarl. "Is that any way to talk to your next prince?"

I scoff. "You're lying."

"I'm not!" Her voice reaches a sudden pitch that surprises me. Nathan goes rigid in her lap, his eyes wide. She collects herself, grips his tiny arms, and then says, "He *is* the rightful heir. You'll see."

It makes me sick, the way she's spewing these lies right in front of the little boy. "That's not possible."

"Isn't it? You don't *know* what Roland and I shared." She scoffs and plays with Nathan's hair, untwisting a curl. "You don't think you're the first, do you? Oh, no. There was a time when *I* was their little princess."

If the chloroform doesn't make me sick, that might. I take small sips of water and try not to heave again.

The door opens suddenly, and for a second hope surges through me. It's dashed, however, when I see Imogen's brother holding on to the handle. "There's someone at the door," he says. "What do you want me to do about it?"

"Go take a look," she says, and her eyes scan over to me. "We have nothing to hide." She lifts Nathan and sets him on the floor. "Go with your uncle, dear."

Using the child as a human shield? It makes me queasy

again. Nathan walks to his uncle and takes the older man's hand.

"Oh…Rory." Imogen curls forward, eyes narrowing at me. Her bag is on the floor, and she lifts a small pistol out of it. The sight makes my heart hammer. "If you scream," she says, "I'll put one in your belly." The look in her eyes say she *might* be mad enough to do it. I seal my mouth shut. Imogen stands, goes to a stereo, and turns it on. Opera music swells through the room and leaves my ears ringing.

Then she comes back to me and grabs the rope. "Hands above your head, dear," she says, gun pointing at me still, so I comply.

25

ROLAND

"*I*t looks closed, mate."

I've got my hand cupped over my eyes as I peer into the dark abyss of Three Swans dance studio. Benjamin is waiting by the car; Sam is in the back in case someone tries to make a run for it. Inside, there's a reception desk, rolled-up yoga mats, and large swaths of red fabric hanging from the ceilings. I can also see a door behind the desk, which must lead to the rest of the studio. But the front door is locked, and the lights are out.

"Are you sure?" Ben asks.

"Wait—hold on. Someone's coming."

A lumbering shadow of a figure comes out of the door behind the reception desk, closing it behind him. I stand back when he approaches, unlocks the front door, and holds it ajar. He's an unhappy-looking man, with a frown made for a bass fish.

I recognize him immediately. He's the man from the video—Rory's captor. Arthur Dodds. My chest tightens.

"We're closed," he grunts.

I remind myself that he doesn't know that I know who he is. I have to play this cool if I want to get inside. "Hi." I force a smile and stick out my hand. "Prince Roland. Mind if we step inside, mate?"

The *prince* bit usually opens any door. This bulldog of a man is the first I've seen to look unimpressed. But then a small voice says with a gasp, "A *real* prince?"

I look down. There's a young boy huddled behind the man's legs. He has a mop of blond hair, a little suit on, and wide, shining eyes.

Arthur looks irritated but then does open the door. Assuming the quicker we're in, the quicker we're out, I suppose. "What's this all about, then?" he asks.

"We're looking for a missing person," Ben interjects. He reaches into his pocket and pulls out his phone. When he lands on a picture of Rory, he holds it over for the man to look at. "Does this woman look familiar?"

Arthur squints at the picture, then shakes his head. "No. Can't say I've seen her before."

There's a low thump of music coming from the closed door. "Is someone else here?"

"It's a private lesson," Arthur explains.

"We need to speak with the owner," Ben presses. "Imogen Dodds. Is she around?"

He shakes his head. "No." He's lying. His eyes flicker around the room nervously.

I clear my throat. "Well. Perhaps we could get your name and number. In case we need to reach out to you later."

He scowls but then plucks a card from the reception desk and hands it over to Ben. "Here you go. Now I've got to get back—"

"Arthur Dodds," Ben reads off the card. "What, not Gideon Calder today?"

Now a flush rises up the man's face. He grips the little boy's shoulder, holding the kid close, and my heart skips a beat, suddenly nervous for the kid. I don't want to push him, not while there's a little boy around. "What of it?" Arthur growls. "Sometimes I use a fake name to take pictures. Sell them to magazines. Not a crime, is it?"

"No," Ben says, his voice like steel. "But kidnapping is."

I crouch down so I'm level with the boy. "Hey," I tell him. "You have any toys around here? I'd love to see them."

The boy nods and squirms out of the man's grip, rushing to a corner closet. "Right in here!" he says excitedly, gripping the doorknob. I help him out with it, opening it up to a small closet stuffed with props.

Which is when Ben strikes. I see him out of the corner of my eye—he swings at Arthur and knocks the other man off his feet. The boy starts to turn around to the noise of their struggle, but I quickly grip his small shoulders and crouch down beside him, fitting us both into the closet so he can't see the violence outside. "What'd you say your name was, mate?"

"Um." He looks nervous now. I can hear Arthur grunt and swear before Ben pulls the other man into a chokehold and cups his mouth. I plaster a smile on my face and draw the boy's focus on me, adjusting my body in the doorframe. "I'm...Nathan."

"Nathan. It's nice to meet you. Is your mum around?"

"This is my bag of jacks," he explains, ignoring my question as he pulls a little bag out of a cubby. He opens the drawstrings and spills jacks over the floor. "I play them when I get bored."

"Fascinating. Show me how it works." Out of the corner of my eye, Ben is struggling to keep his hold on Arthur. The other man elbows him in the gut, and I wince as Ben doubles over. I nearly go to help, but—Ben has this. And I need to keep Nathan out of the fray.

Sure enough, Ben grabs on to one of the hanging aerial silks. He hooks it around the other man's throat and pulls. Tight. Arthur still puts up a fight, but he's weakening now, slumping against Ben.

"I'm not very good at catching them," Nathan says, snapping my attention back on him.

"I think you're brilliant," I tell him.

Nathan's eyes scan over me, and his little eyebrows furrow. "Are you sure you're a real prince?" he asks.

"Pretty sure, mate. Why?"

"Am I?"

"Are you what?"

"Roland." Ben is behind me suddenly. His hand touches my shoulder. "We have to move."

I glance behind him. Arthur is horizontal on the floor. I can see his boots sticking motionless out from behind the desk. "Is he…?"

"Unconscious. But not for long."

"Nathan—" I turn to the boy. I take out my phone and open up a picture of Rory, holding it out for him. "Have you seen this woman around here?"

He looks at the picture, then at the floor. "Uh-huh."

"It's important, buddy. Do you know where she is?"

He pushes his hair back from his forehead, screws his mouth up, and then points to the door where the music is coming from.

My heart hammers in my chest. I'm terrified to think of what state I'll find Rory in. There's a small bulb on a string in the closet, so I turn on the light. "Do you think you can stay in here?" I ask Nathan. "And play your jacks for a little bit? I'll be right back to get you, all right, mate?"

"Okay," he says, as though my request is completely sensible.

I get to my feet and gently close the closet door. It's not ideal, but the kid is safe. For now.

I glance at Ben. I'm a nervous wreck, but he's calm as glass, which quells my nerves a bit. We both turn to the door, the haunting sounds of thin operatic voices coming from it.

"Let's get this over with," Ben says.

I reach out and touch my fingers to the doorknob. Slowly, I turn it. It's not locked and it clicks open. My hands are shaking as I ease the door open. Inside, I see polished wood floors. Mirrored walls.

And Rory. Slumped against the wall, her hands bound to the horizonal pole above her. Her wedding dress spills over the floor, and when she looks up at me, her hair falls over her face, but I can still see the relief light up those sea-green eyes.

"Roland!" she cries out in warning.

I rush through the door, towards her. Just then, the door slams shut behind me. I whirl around. *Imogen*. She's just as I remembered her—long, raven hair, lithe frame, Cheshire cat smile. Except her eyes are wild in a way they never were before.

"So nice of you to join us, my prince," she purrs. She has a pistol in her hand, and it's aimed at me.

Ben is locked out on the other side of the door. He's pounding on it, shouting my name. But she locks it and jams a chair against the handle. It's going to take a lot more than brute force for him to get in now.

I'm trapped in here with a madwoman, and Rory. Ben is the one with the gun and the soldier skills required to fight his way out of this mess. Me? All I've got is my mind, so I try to focus my thoughts away from the barrel of her gun.

"Imogen." I say her name and slowly lift my palms so she can see I mean her no harm. "It's been a while, hasn't it?"

"Too long," she says. "I've been waiting for you…for so long."

"You have me," I say, lifting my arms at my sides. "So let's talk. Just the two of us. Let Rory go."

My gaze flickers back to Rory again. She looks like she's in some sort of daze, and I want so badly to scoop her up, to kiss her, to tell her it will be all right.

But Imogen's mouth suddenly turns cruel. "I can't do that," she says simply. "That slut is the reason for all…*this*."

Then she turns the gun on Rory. Fear rips through me, and my heart hammers in my chest. "What do you want, Imogen?"

She nods to the table. "The truth," she says. "Sit."

I take a seat. The setup is strange: there's a tripod across from me with a camera sitting up top, a thin black wire attaching it to a laptop. Imogen circles around the table and then turns to the camera and starts to fiddle with it.

I take the opportunity to look at Rory. "Rory. Are you okay?"

Rory smiles weakly. "Never better."

"Don't talk to her!" Imogen hisses, so I go quiet. As she aims the camera at me, she says, "Do you know where I was…the day that ghastly sex tape came out with you and the American bitch, Roland? I was at home. Taking care of *our* son. You met him, didn't you?"

"Nathan," I say, my voice hollow in my own ears. "He's your boy?"

"*Our* boy," she corrects. "Born on November seventh, nine months after our beautiful, passionate night. You remember that night, don't you?"

"I do," I tell her. But my mouth is dry.

She laughs—a weird, stilted sound. "I think about it… every day. And now we're going to make a movie of our own. As soon as I start filming…everything from this camera goes live online. And once it's out there…there's no taking it back."

There's a knot in my throat. But Rory looks like she's fighting consciousness, Ben is slamming on the door, and I need to buy them some time. So if she wants to make a video —fine. Let's make a video. "What do you want me to say?" I ask.

"The *truth*," she says. There's a real feverish look in her eyes now, and even as she looks through the camera, she keeps the gun trained on Rory. "Tell them that this marriage was a mistake…that you love me and you've always loved me. And our son…Nathan…is your only true and rightful heir." She smiles. It's a twisted smile. "Can you do that?"

Time. I need more time. "Perhaps we should discuss this. Get my script straight."

But her frown returns. "No," she says. "If you say the wrong thing…I'll kill her. Does that work for you, Your Majesty?"

My chest is tight. I can hardly breathe. "I'll say it," I tell her. "The truth."

Her eyes shine at that. "Good boy." Then she flicks a button on the camera and a tiny, red light blares at me. It's recording.

I take in a shaky breath. I feel like a naked man on stage. My hands are trembling, but I know I can't—I won't—mess this up. So I clear my throat and say, "My name is Prince Roland. I'm…here to clear up some…misconceptions."

Time, I think. *Buy yourself time.* Imogen's eyes are glued on me expectantly; she's no longer focused on Rory. Which is good. So I continue. "Years ago…before I met Rory…I was lonely. Locked away in Helmsway Palace. I had no way of… meeting people. So I'd send my bodyguard, Ben, to find a suitable woman and bring her to the palace. I'm not…particularly proud of my actions. I was immature then. These… women…they provided comfort. Companionship. Sometimes more. One in particular…Imogen Dodds…was quite special. I met her in the winter—January, maybe February, I think…it was cold in the evenings, I remember that…"

Imogen steps away from the tripod. Out of sight of the camera, she presses the barrel of the gun to the top of Rory's head, and she mouths, "Get to the point."

I swallow hard and my words nearly trip over my tongue. "The point is…I've kept her a secret for some time, but the truth of the matter is, I love her. And I want to be with her." An idea clicks, and I force a smile and reach out. "In fact…I want to introduce her to the world right now. Imogen, please, come here."

Imogen wavers. I can see the hesitation in her eyes. *Come!* I want to scream. *Get away from Rory!*

Instead, I widen my smile and motion again. "Please, my love."

Finally, her shoulders relax. Her arm drops to her side, hiding the gun from view. And she seems to walk on air as she approaches me, her smile growing as she gets closer. Her fingers touch mine, and I take her hand, pulling it to my mouth to give it a kiss. And then, I lay it on thick: "This is the woman I love...Princess Imogen."

It's the very words she needs to hear, apparently, because all the harshness in her face melts. At once, she *almost* looks like the woman I remember from before—a softer, gentler version of herself. She slips her hand over my face, and her touch sends chills through me. It takes everything inside of me not to recoil, but I grind my teeth as she traces my jawline. *Every second is another second Rory is alive*, I tell myself. *Keep her alive.*

"Roland," she sighs, "my prince has come back to me."

She leans forward and I realize then that she's going to kiss me. My bones go rigid, and my skin crawls as her thumb strokes my cheek. Her breath hits my face, her eyes fall closed, and then—

"Roland, duck."

Imogen's eyes snap open, and we both look up to see—

Rory. Unbound. Standing beside us, holding the tripod up above her head. I lean out of the way just in time as Rory swings it, the camera smashing hard into the back of Imogen's head. Imogen stands, her mouth opened, dazed. So Rory swings again. This time, it collides with her temple and the camera smashes to bits. Imogen crumples to the floor, out cold.

Rory's breathing is labored. She drops the tripod and

sways on her feet. Immediately, I jump up and grab her, just as she starts to slide. "Rory," I say quickly. "Are you hurt?"

"She ties worse knots than I do," Rory mumbles. She's slumped against me, her eyelids fluttering, and we both sink to the ground.

I cradle her, my Rory, soft and warm and *alive* in my arms. "It's okay," I tell her. "Everything's going to be okay."

And everything is. The door finally snaps off its hinges, and when it flies open, I can see reinforcements have arrived. Ben and Sam are there, along with a handful of members from our security team.

Immediately, Ben makes a beeline to us. "Are you two okay?" he asks, panic evident in his eyes.

"Ben…" Rory sobs his name. She reaches out and clings to us, both of us, one hand on me, the other on Ben.

"Call a doctor," I tell him. So he does.

26

BEN

*T*his scene feels all too familiar.

I'm sitting in a private waiting room, Roland beside me. All the other chairs are empty, the room cleared for royalty. There's a stack of magazines beside me and a fake plant in the corner. Rory is a couple of doors down the hall from us. The doctors whisked her away as soon as we got to the hospital, promising they'd send someone over with an update.

But that was nearly thirty minutes ago, and I can't imagine what's taken so damned long. My stomach feels like it's been twisted up in knots. I'm worried about Rory. I'm worried about the baby. I'm terrifying Imogen has done irrevocable damage to one or both of them…and there's not a fucking thing I can do except sit here and wait.

There's a TV hanging from the ceiling, and it's been blaring the news since we sat down. They're repeating the same stories over and over, and none of the newscasters can make any sense of it. They talk about the royal wedding that turned into a royal disaster. They talk about the mysterious video that leaked with Prince Roland confessing his love for another woman. And then they discuss rumors that alleged mistress Imogen Dodds has been taken in by the authorities, but for what, no one's certain.

"Will someone turn that bloody thing off?" Roland snaps —the first thing he's said since we got here.

I get up, climb on a chair, and reach the knob to turn the television off. Not because it's bothering much, but because it gives me something to do, at least. When I step back down, Roland lets out a pained noise and clutches himself.

"This is my fault," he says.

I ease back down in the seat beside him. "You had no idea there was a madwoman after you."

"No—but it *is* my fault," he protests. "All my...bloody secrets. Trying to keep things quiet. It was bound to blow up on my face one way or another, I just...I didn't think it would come to this."

I worry my bottom lip between my teeth. "Imogen was in love with someone she couldn't have," I say. "It's enough to drive anyone mad. I should know."

Roland casts me a dark look at that. "Are you defending her?"

"No," I say firmly. "I just...think we should call it what it is. She's mental. Hopefully she's someplace where she can get the help she needs."

Roland goes quiet for a moment. Finally, he asks, "What about Nathan?"

"Who?"

"The...Imogen's little boy." Roland wrings his hands. "If he's mine..."

"If he's yours," I interrupt, "then you claim him. He'd be your son. He's an innocent in all this."

"I know," Roland says quickly. But the look of concern doesn't leave his face. This isn't how he thought fatherhood would go.

To ease his pain, I add, "We also don't know that he is

yours. We were both in that bed with her. That's an equally likely chance he could be mine."

"Don't think either of you are gonna have to worry about that," Benjamin's voice announces as he enters the room. He's all gangly limbs with a dumb grin planted on his face. When he sees my glare, however, his smile drops just a little. "Sorry, boss. Didn't mean to eavesdrop. But…I think you two may want to see this."

Roland and I exchange a look before we get to our feet and follow Benjamin down the hall. He leads us out to the main lobby. We hang at the edge, by the doorframe. I spot Nathan then, the worried little boy who's anxiously picking at a stuffed animal someone gave him. He's sitting beside a policeman, who looks like he's doing his best to entertain the boy. But then a man and a woman enter the lobby, escorted by another policeman. Nathan sees them and his stuffed animal falls to the floor, forgotten.

"Mummy!" he shouts and leaps out of his chair, racing across the room. His mother falls to her knees and scoops him into a tight hug. His father joins in, and they're crying, laughing, hugging, and she keeps saying, *My baby, my precious boy*.

"His name isn't *Nathan Dodds*," Benjamin fills us in. "It's Nathan Easterly. His parents reported him missing nearly a week ago. Apparently, they take his sister to ballet classes at Three Swans. He came with them one day, dad left him alone for only a minute to help his sister into her uniform, and then—poof. Little Nathan was gone. Running theory is, Imogen fixated on the boy because he looks enough like a Pennington, and her brother kidnapped him then and there. The police are working out the details, but—"

"But right now, all that matters is that they're reunited," I say.

Watching them together—the Easterlys—it tugs at my heartstrings a little too hard. Was there part of me that *wanted* Nathan to be ours? Is my biological clock ticking that badly?

No—it's something else. They're a family. United. Our family—our strange little trio—has been fractured and bruised. Right now, I'm craving that feeling of togetherness.

Maybe Roland feels it, too, because he lets out a heavy sigh beside me. "Nathan found his family," Roland says. I feel his hand on my shoulder then. He squeezes. "We have to go back to ours."

* * *

RORY LOOKS UNBEARABLY small in her hospital bed.

She has an IV in one arm, her hair is knotted, and she looks so tired. They've taken her out of her wedding dress and packed her into a band shirt that swallows her. She's sitting up, though, so that's good, and when she sees us, a small smile slides over her mouth. "Hi…"

"Rory—" Roland's voice is hoarse with emotion, and he rushes to her side. He takes her hand in his and draws her hair back. "Bloody hell, you gave us a scare. Are you okay?"

I want to hold her, embrace her, but something keeps me at bay, as though there are invisible strings holding me back. So I stand at the end of her bed instead, watching them.

"I'm fine…" Rory says, and gives us a small smile. "The baby is fine, too."

"Thank God," I breathe.

Rory's gaze turns to me then, and her eyes shimmer. "Nathan…is he okay?"

"He's fine," I tell her quickly. "Safe. It turns out…he's been missing from his family…his *real* family…for days. Imogen snatched him up, just like she did you."

Rory looks shaken. "That's terrible…"

"Children are resilient," I reassure her. "I don't think he

143

understood much of it. Probably thought it was a strange game."

"I hope so," Rory whispers. Her hand falls to her stomach protectively.

But Roland isn't so easy comforted. He starts speaking quickly. "Rory—I'm so sorry. All those people at the wedding, and not one of us were able to stop him from taking you—"

"The wedding," Rory says in a soft, shocked voice, as though she's just remembered it. Then she looks like she might cry. "It's...no one's fault but mine. I bolted. Through one of the hidden staircases. Everything was set for the wedding...everyone was waiting for me...*you* were waiting for me and I...I just panicked..."

"The wedding was a rubbish idea, Rory," Roland cuts her off firmly. "It didn't feel right."

Rory's lower lip trembles. She covers her mouth, but she can't stop the sob that escapes. "Thank you," she chokes out.

"For what?"

"For just...ugh. *Saying* it!" She wipes tears away from her cheeks. "God. We both felt it, and neither of us wanted to say a damn thing. If she hadn't taken me, would we have just gone through with it?"

Roland shakes his head. "I'm not sure."

"Well, there's your silver lining." Rory makes a sweeping motion with her hand as though shoving away all the bad thoughts. "That's it. No hiding things from each other. No secrets. We used to tell each other everything...I don't know when that stopped. I'm including myself in that, by the way. I could have told the both of you about the baby much sooner...instead, I hid from the two men who love me more than anything." She sniffles and then says, sadly, "A tissue, please."

My heart breaks. I snatch up a box of tissues and hold it out for her. She takes one and blows her nose hard. I feel things left unsaid burning a hole like acid in my trachea.

Finally I can't take it anymore and clear my throat uncomfortably. "Since we're...putting everything out in the open."

Rory blinks at me with watery eyes. "What is it?"

I shift my weight from one foot to the other. "Well...that night that we spent at my parents' flat. We got on the boat. And..." My tongue knots itself. Oh, bloody hell. *Spit it out.* A bit too forcefully, I say, "And I was planning to propose to you that night." I glance at Roland and back at Rory. "Both of you. Had the rings and everything."

Roland looks stunned. "Ben..." he says softly. "Why didn't you?"

God, that look in his eyes makes me want to hide my head in the sand and never come out. But I stand my ground. "It didn't matter," I say firmly. "I stand by my decision...that the baby will be better off as a Pennington."

"*Your* decision." Rory says the words slowly, bitterly. Then she points. "Ben. Do you see that newspaper over there?"

I follow her finger. "Yes."

"Bring it."

Not sure if now's the time to catch up on the daily, but I follow her request. I pick the paper and bring it over to her. Rory rolls it up, then proceeds to whap me on the top of the head with it, as though I'm a dog that's just pissed on her carpet. It doesn't hurt, but it is annoying, and I wince all the same.

"*Bad*," she says, jabbing the paper in my direction. Then she turns to Roland and repeats the action on his head.

"What'd I do?" he protests.

"We can't keep doing this. You—" She points the paper at me. "—made a decision for the group without sharing with us. And you—" Now it's Roland's turn. "—were willing to go along with something that made you uncomfortable just because you thought it was what we wanted. I'm not perfect, either. I know that. But we're not going to make it if we're not honest with each other."

Rory lets out an exhausted sigh. She lowers her weapon (thank God) and laces her fingers with mine, and her other hand with Roland's. "So…let's stop doing what everyone else wants and start doing what *we* want. We've always been better like that. And everything else will fall into place. It always does. Let's make a pact, here and now…no more secrets. Whatever future we decide on…we have to decide on it *together*."

Her words are surprisingly cathartic. A weight I didn't realize I'd been carrying lifts from my shoulders. I squeeze her hand and say, "I can agree to that."

"Me too," Roland says quickly.

"Good," Rory says. And the smile on her face is so sweet, it makes my chest lift. "So. Let's talk."

And we do. We talk for hours. We take turns vocalizing our thoughts, hopes, and fears about the future. The trials of being a triad, fears of being an inadequate parent, clinging to old traditions…we talk about it all. Roland admits that the pressures of being a royal occasionally weigh on him, and he's afraid of disappointing his people and—yes—his queen mother. Rory opens up about her fears of settling down, her worries that she'll never be satisfied if she can't travel at the drop of a dime.

And I confess the demons on my shoulder. My fear of being abandoned or outcasted and my bad habit of hurting my own feelings before anyone else can. I hate talking about my emotions, but this haven we've created after the whirlwind of today feels like a safe place. Maybe we're all just adrenaline high and exhausted, but whatever the straw is that breaks the camel's back, it becomes evident that we needed this. All three of us.

Nurses come in and out every now and then, only briefly interrupting the flow of our conversation before we dive back in. Visiting hours are up, but Roland is the prince of England, and no one's worked up the nerve to tell us to leave yet. I'm sitting on the hospital bed beside Rory, my arm around her back, and Roland is sprawled over both of us with his head in my lap, her fingers petting his thick hair.

"I want to see them," Rory says and turns to me. "The rings you got for us."

I press my lips together. "I don't have them on me."

Rory gasps. "What…they're not stashed in some secret pocket in your blazer?"

"They're in my office. I'll show you when we're back home."

I rub my hand over the bare side of her throat, and she nuzzles tighter against my shoulder. "I think…I still want to get married," she says. "*Ish.*"

I squint at her. "What does that mean?"

"I mean…I know it won't be legal or anything. But that doesn't matter. I want…a ceremony. Something to celebrate the three of us."

"A *we*-dding," Roland says. "Brilliant." The three of us chuckle.

"I'd love that." I squeeze her shoulder.

Rory continues, "I just…think about Ben's family. And my family. They don't need a crown or a title to be happy. And… yeah. I understand that a royal bloodline is a big deal. I'm fine with that. But I don't think this baby needs all that… hanging over their shoulders. Not until they're ready, anyway."

Roland shrugs. "My mum's an ice queen, my father is dead, and my aunt's in prison. The bloodline isn't all it's cracked up to be."

Rory says carefully, "I just think…we don't need to be something we're not. This baby doesn't need a crown to have a good life. He—or she—just needs to be loved."

"If we have anything," Roland says, reaching up to tug the scruff of my beard, "it's an abundance of love."

147

"Exactly." Rory tucks her head on my shoulder. "So let's not do anything to divide that ever again."

"What did you have in mind?" Roland asks. "For the ceremony, that is."

I roll the thought around my tongue before finally uttering, "I might have an idea."

27

RORY

*I*taly is beautiful this time of year.

Though—to be fair—I don't think there's a time of year that Italy *isn't* beautiful. The crystal-blue coast. Trees that birth lemons as big as my head. Buildings the color of sea glass that stack along the coast. The Leon d'Oro is a Moorish villa that hangs off the Sorrento cliffs. It's tucked away behind red clay and thick trees but impossible to miss. It's owned by the Pennington family—has been in their family for generations—and had fallen into disrepair until recently, when Roland took up the task of renovating the place.

Although we started—and continue—the majority of our relationship in the walls of Helmsway Palace, I still think of this building as the place where we really found our groove as a trouple. It was the first time we were able to separate from everyone else and just *be*. What we found here was so beautiful, so real, and so fiery hot it's a miracle we didn't turn the beach sands into glass.

It feels right that we start our next chapter here.

The media frenzy has only finally started to die down around us. After I left the hospital, Roland held a press conference to tell the story—the real story—of everything that happened the day of our wedding. He confessed everything. How he and Ben used to share women at the palace, and how Imogen had been just one of many. How she and her brother had worked together to kidnap me and hold me hostage. And how the video had been a ruse to get me out alive. He explains that no, there won't be another wedding between just him and I. Yes, he, Ben, and I are very much in love. And people can love it or hate it, but he won't be quiet about it anymore.

His admission has a strange affect. At first, there's the familiar swell of hatred. People spewing insults, calling us heathens, and saying we *deserved* what Imogen had done. People calling Roland and Ben players and perverts. But then women start coming out—women previously silenced by their NDAs. Women who spent the night at the palace with Ben and Roland and come out in defense of the men. They're all different types of women—younger, older, from all parts of the country. In interviews, they all repeat the same lines. The threesomes were consensual. Roland and Ben were gentlemen. And—as I very well know—they were beasts in bed.

"God *forbid* women enjoy their own sexuality," one woman—get this, a *duchess*—comments dryly in an interview. "First they tell us we can't say *no*, now we can't say *yes*, either. Some women want to be dominated. Some want to be worshipped. And, yes, some of us quite like the idea of two gorgeous men kissing all over us. Whatever we want, we should be allowed to take it without shame. Greedy girls have more fun, after all."

That's the line that really hits—*Greedy girls have more fun*. It's printed on T-shirts. Mugs. The press starts calling them the *Royal Mistresses*, and suddenly, everyone wants to be a mistress.

Our relationship—which was previously tucked in the

shadows—explodes into light. And now *everyone* wants to know how it works. And not in a bad way, either. They stop hating us and start wanting to *be* us. There are makeup tutorials online to show you how to get that "Rory March glow." A clothing store tailored for queer and non-binary folks comes out with a line of watches with the tagline "Be the man for who the Ben Tolles..."—which I, personally, have no idea what that means, but Roland and I get a kick out of it.

It could be worse. But it's funny—now that we're in the spotlight, we're craving our own space. Everyone wants to know if we're going to have another ceremony, but one for the three of us this time. Are we going to raise the baby together? Who's going to be "Daddy"? We're no longer a scandal—now, we're a phenomenon. Even *Saturday Night Live* does a skit about us. We're *that* normal.

Without telling anyone, we planned out our own small, private ceremony. Roland had the Leon set up before we even stepped foot into it, and I should've known he would make it *extra*. Crystal champagne flutes are lined up on the kitchen counter for the after-party, presents are piled in the corner (even though Roland encouraged everyone to donate to the Cystic Fibrosis Foundation in lieu of gifts), and the floor is clean enough to eat off. Outside on the patio, the ivy hedge to keep prying eyes out is thick and trimmed, the pool has been cleaned and decorated with a line of candles around the rim, and an arch has been set up at the very edge of the patio, by the wrought iron fence, overlooking the deep sea and the waning sun.

The sky is streaked with purples, pinks, and oranges, and the same colors ripple over the stretch of water. Our small crew of close family and friends have congregated around the pool, and when I look out, I recognize my parents, Ben's family, and a couple friends from the States and from my travels. Sam is there, of course, wearing her full black suit even in the balmy Italian summer, and she gives me a *you've got this, girl* wink when my eyes land on her.

While her reassurance is appreciated, it's not needed. The day of my wedding to Roland, I went into a full panic attack. But I've had nothing but happy butterflies all day waiting for *this moment*.

I'm not wearing white—I mean, c'mon, who thinks I'm a virgin at this point? Instead, I picked this beautiful, light-blue wedding dress, that—miracle of miracles—fits my baby belly, which is now melon-size. I'm standing under the arch, and Roland and Ben walk at the same time on either side of the pool to meet me in the center.

Can I say they look dapper? They look dapper as hell. They're both in matching black suits, but with traces of the same blue from my wedding dress—Roland's tie is blue, and Ben has a blue pocket square in his blazer. Roland looks in his element, all white smiles and perfectly coiffed hair. Ben— bless him—is so awkward right now. He hates eyes on him, and it's painfully obvious, the way he stands with his hands laced together in front of his groin.

I try Sam's trick. I slip my hands in theirs, breaking up Ben's grip in the process. I give his hand a squeeze, and when he looks at me, I flash him a wink. "Relax," I whisper. "This is the fun part."

It seems to work, because a small smile edges up the corner of his mouth and his shoulders lose their stiffness.

"You look hot, mate," Roland says to him, urging him to loosen up a little more.

Ben's eyes widen and I can't tell if that's the sunset or a blush climbing his throat. "There's…company, Roland."

"Oh, don't worry about me," my brother says. "I've heard worse."

My brother, Oscar, is easy to miss; he's half everyone's height, sitting in his wheelchair beside me. He looks like me —we have the same untamable red hair, the same button nose—but his skin is lighter, his freckles are most pronounced than mine, and his face is gaunter. The real resemblance, Roland told me once, is in our eyes—we both have this mischievous glint at all times. He looks *amazing*, suited up, with a red blazer that matches our ginger hair. I always knew he was brave, but he's climbed out of his shell completely since our family blew up in the royal media frenzy, one of the few positive side effects of a constant lack of privacy. Oscar is my backbone, and I couldn't imagine this ceremony without him—we'd already agreed that if he couldn't come to us, we'd come to him.

Luckily, he made it. His girlfriend, Francesca, and my parents helped him get here, but only a little—us Marches crave our independence above all. He's our honorary "minister"—which we can do because, well, *none* of this is legal. It's just a celebration. A celebration of love and a commitment to each other that we so very much deserve.

"Should we get this party started?" Oscar asks, glancing between us.

"Please." I grin.

"Very well." Now he faces our small audience, and his voice grows in volume so everyone can hear him. "Ladies, gentlemen, and everyone in between. Thank you for coming. We're here to honor these freaks and geeks. Royals and gents. And my crazy, can't-do-anything-the-normal-way sister."

If people were holding their breath for a traditional ceremony, they let it out now with a burst of surprised laughter.

"I know she's been screaming for attention ever since I was diagnosed with cystic fibrosis, but *really*, this is next level," Oscar continues. Leave it to my older brother to rib me at my own wedding. I roll my eyes dramatically, but even Ben can't help himself from chuckling under his breath.

But then Oscar's voice turns serious. "Speaking of my diagnosis—about five years ago, it got ugly. In that time, I watched Rory sacrifice everything to give me the world. There's nothing more important to her than family. So it didn't surprise me when Rory found Roland and Ben. She wasn't looking for a lover…she was looking for a family. And as I've watched them grow…and endured countless hours of her lovesick gushing over Skype…it seems to be that she's found exactly that."

At his words, my vision starts to blur with tears. I'm trying desperately to hold it together, but a couple slip out. Ben gives me his pocket square so I can dab my eyes, and Roland laces his fingers in my own.

"I've seen my sister grow from a starry-eyed young girl, dragging around a stuffed otter, to a grown-ass woman, who takes on impossible challenges and knock them down. Who *loves* hard—and who has two men who love her and each other equally as hard. So…with all that…it's an honor to celebrate with them today. Here, they're announcing to friends and family their forever-bond…a promise to love each other, support each other, and protect each other, through whatever life may throw at them." Oscar clears his throat. "So…with that. If you have anything to say to one another…now's the time."

"I'll start," Roland says. He reaches out and takes Ben's hand as well, so now he's holding on to both of us. "Rory… you fell into my life and exploded it. You opened my eyes and my world in a way I'll never be able to repay you for…but I plan to spend forever trying. And Ben…never has there been a man so loyal, so patient, and giving. You're part of me, and I don't know myself without you. I never want to know." Roland's hand tightens on mine, his crystal-blue eyes sweeping from me to Ben and back again. "I promise to love the both of you with my whole heart…to prioritize our family, above all things. And I promise not to leave so many crumbs in the bed."

Both Ben and I snort a laugh at that and exchange a look —we'll believe it when we see it.

It's my turn next, so I close the circle, taking Ben's other hand. "God…this is…so insane," I start. "It's been a roller coaster of a ride from day one. In a way…I think it's lucky that our relationship developed the way it did, with all the bumps. We grew up together, in a way…and I've been so, incredibly lucky and proud of both of you." Oh no, the tears. The tears are coming. I take a deep, shuddering breath, overwhelmed by my love for these two, and squeeze their hands, trying to hold it together enough to get through my vows. "We've been on so many adventures together…and I'm so grateful that I found men who don't drag me down or take me away from the things I love, but instead encourage me to reach for the stars and love me for the crazy, wild, and ridiculously clumsy woman I am. You've been the best boyfriends…the best *friends* a woman could ask for…and I can't wait to see you as husbands and fathers. I can't *wait* to see what the future has in store for us."

Thank God I'm done, because now I can sniffle to myself. My two men look glassy-eyed themselves. Until Ben clears his throat, untangles his hands from ours, and reaches into the inner pocket of his blazer. "Sod the both of you for memorizing your lines," he says and pulls out a folded-up paper, which lightens the mood with a much-needed laugh. "Rory," Ben says, his voice clear and firm as his gaze flickers between my eyes and the page in front of him. "My girl. My kitten. You're tenacious. Brave. Genuine—and unapologetically so. I admire you as much as I love you—which is a lot.

"Roland. My prince. Royal pain in the arse. I've loved you from the minute I met you. You're intelligent. Stubborn. And you care very much about everyone around you. Your empathy makes you a good person…and will, one day, make you a great king.

"To both of you—I promise to stand by you. Protect you.

Love you, honor you, and respect you. I also promise to love myself as much as the two of you do—something that, occasionally, can be a challenge for me. You deserve the best version of me, and I vow to give that to you, every day, for the rest of our lives. I love you."

With that, quietly, Ben folds the paper back up into his jacket.

I can't stop it anymore—tears of happiness, gratitude, and love slip down my cheeks. Even my brother sniffles beside me. Is he fighting back tears of his own? I don't think I've ever seen my brother cry, but if he does, I'm definitely going to break down sobbing.

"Psst!" Ben's niece, our ring bearer in her pretty princess dress, tugs on Ben's pant leg and holds up a box. "Don't forget these!"

"Thank you, monkey," he says and musses her hair before taking the box.

"Right," Oscar says, quickly wiping his face. "The rings. That's important. You should probably…do that."

As rehearsed, we do this in the order our relationship started: Ben slips my ring on, touches my face, and his lips gently kiss mine. I drop my hand on Roland's shoulder, down his arm, and take his ring out of the box, sliding it over his finger before I kiss him, feeling his soft, warm mouth envelop mine.

When, lastly, Roland puts Ben's ring on and they kiss, my heart does this silly little backflip.

"By the power vested in me by no one," Oscar says, "I now pronounce you husbands and wife."

Our little crowd cheers and hoots. My heart skips in my chest, and I lean against Roland. I can't stop smiling. "Did we really do that?" I whisper.

"We certainly did." Ben grins back at me.

We step off the altar as our friends clap for us. Queen Selena kisses me on the forehead, then touches Ben's shoulder and tells us she's happy for us. My parents, who I haven't seen in so long, race over to hug me. Everyone surrounds us, embracing us, shaking hands, congratulating us.

"All right, three cheers for them!" Sam cups her hand and shouts. "Prince Roland, Princess Rory, and Prince Ben!"

There are shouts and a smattering of applause, and I break into laughter. It doesn't *matter* what's "official" or "by the book." People are going to see what they want to see. And they're going to love Roland—and us—for being brave enough to be ourselves.

The rest of the ceremony is a complete whirlwind. We have food set up inside, and people grab what they want and then enjoy drinks outside, under the twinkling night stars. Ben, Roland, and I spend most of the time chatting with our guests. There are people here from the United States that I haven't seen in *eons*, and it's really, really good to catch up. We've set speakers up outside, and after everyone's got a couple of drinks in them, it turns into a dance party. I'm hyped up, on an adrenaline high, so I join the fray, dancing with friends until Roland swoops in, his arm around my back. Then I dance with him, and before I know it, Ben is behind me, his hands at my hips, and I feel so loved, so *complete* with the two of them.

Before I'm ready for it to, the party winds down. It's the early hours of morning by the time I realize I haven't eaten. There's still some wedding cake left, so I sneak away with a plate and a fork. I slip upstairs to our bedroom, knowing none of the drunk stragglers will stumble up here. My feet hurt from dancing so much, even though I took my shoes off halfway through the night and have dirty toes to prove it. I should take off my dress, wash up, but I don't want the spell of tonight to end, so instead I sit down on the edge of the bed and enjoy my cake alone.

But I'm not alone for long. The door opens and I see Ben,

surprise in his eyes, cake on his plate.

"I see I didn't have an original idea," he says.

I pat the spot on the bed beside me. "Come join the party."

"Don't mind if I do."

We sit side by side, shoulders brushing and forks clinking. Finally, the third musketeer flies in—Roland comes bursting through the door, hair wild, smile crooked.

"There you are—thought you two ran away."

"Too far of a swim," Ben teases.

Roland points to our plates. "Oy! Where did you find cake?"

"In the kitchen," Ben says. "Where cake lives."

"C'mon, then. Scoot over and share."

Ben scoots, I share. Roland settles in between us, and we devour the slices like animals.

"Did you hear Sam?" I ask as I suck frosting from my thumb.

Ben says, "You mean when she told Benjamin to *shake his money maker*?"

"Not that—she called you *Prince Ben*." I grin. "I haven't heard that one before."

Now that we're inside, he can't blame the sunset on his reddening ears. "Me neither," Ben mumbles. "It's daft."

"I quite like it." When Ben glares at Roland, Roland sighs. "Come now, my moody little prince…"

"I'm not your prince," Ben corrects flatly.

"No."

"No. If you're going to call me anything—" And now Ben's fingers slip through Roland's thick hair and take a handful. "—you can call me your king."

When Ben's mouth clashes against Roland's, it unleashes a beast that's lain dormant between the three of us. We've been *waiting* for this—to consummate our marriage. Roland groans in his mouth—a low, lusty sound—and I'm immediately wet.

Since I saw them in their suits, I've wanted nothing more than to rip the shirts straight off their chests, and now's my chance. I peel Ben's blazer from his shoulders before gripping his shirt and yanking it from his pants so I can slip my fingers underneath. I kiss his back and touch his sides, the furnace heat of his skin. Ben reaches behind, hooks an arm around my middle, and pulls me around in one swift swoop. I'm between them now—lying against Roland's chest, my gaze locked on the darkness of Ben's eyes, and when he kisses me, it's hungry, rough, and his stubble scrapes my cheek.

Each to their own—but I'm no virgin to be deflowered tonight. They claimed me in front of everyone when they put their ring on my hand, and now I want them to claim me *here*, in our bed, with their tongues and their teeth and their cocks.

We don't waste time. I yank off Ben's belt and undo his pants. He's so hard already, so big and stiff, and when I pull it out and run my fingers over the smooth skin, he growls, "Your panties are nice—take them off before I rip them."

I bite my lip against a grin and pull my dress up my hips —another reason I love this dress: everything is just so much more accessible. I pull my panties down, off one leg, then the other. As soon as they're gone, Ben is on me, hooking my leg around his hip and using the tip of his manhood to spread my nether lips. They're already so slick, so eager, and I gasp as he teases me here, the meaty head of him nuzzling against my buzzing clit. But soon after, he pushes himself inside of me, and I tighten my leg around him because I *need* it, I need to feel him this deep, I need to feel this full.

My head falls back against Roland's shoulder, and I whimper. Roland pulls my hair back, and I feel him work the zipper of my dress. Ben is already in me, already thrusting as Roland takes the hem of my dress. I stretch my arms up and he pulls it over my head, freeing me from the cumbersome

159

fabric. I feel him shift, and he must have undone his own shirt because then his warm chest meets my back, the hairs there tickling my shoulder blades. He kisses my throat, and his hands reach around me, cupping my breasts, playing with my pebbled nipples, before he slides his hand down the bump of my stomach and finds the trimmed thatch of hair between my thighs. I squirm to meet Ben's thrusts and to reach for Roland's hand, but he keeps it painfully just out of reach, just playing with my hair, caressing the outer lips of my sex.

"You're such a good kitten, you know that?" Roland murmurs in my ear, his hot breath beating my throat.

"Thank you, sir," I whimper, delirious with want.

He slips his hand farther down—thank God—and finally hits my swollen little clit. As Ben fucks me, hard, sending explosions of pleasure through my body, Roland paints small, deliberate circles around my sensitive nub because he knows *exactly* how I like it. And just like that, I'm lost to them. I shout—one hand reaching behind me to grip Roland's hair, the other in front of me to dig my nails into Ben's chest, bracing myself against my two rough, dominant, loving men as my orgasm explodes.

I clench around Ben's cock, over and over with heart-beat pulses. He remains iron hard and I savor him, the thickness of him, and he kisses and nibbles my chest as I swoon.

I'm still in the throes of it when—all at once, as though they *synchronized* it—Ben rolls over and Roland flips sides. I let out a yelp of surprise, empty now that Ben's cock has left me, but not for long. I'm crushed between the two of them and loving it as I feel Roland shrug out of the rest of his clothes. Finally, there's nothing but skin between us. Roland's fingers go through my hair, collect it, and then wrap it around his fist. The tightness in my skull makes me see stars, and I sip in a sharp breath, loving the ache.

Roland's hands cup the roundness of my ass, savoring it.

I'm on my hands and knees now, on top of Ben, as Roland presses himself inside of me.

I groan and immediately rock back against him, taking him in deeper. Ben fucks like a machine, but Roland rolls against me like the smooth waves of the ocean, and it's perfect because this is what I need when I'm still so raw, so sensitive, still coming down from my first high.

"You're beautiful," Ben murmurs to me.

Just as Roland says, "You feel so bloody good."

And I let it wash over me, the praise of my men, their love and adoration.

"You're amazing," I whimper. "Both of you…"

My wolf, my lion, and me—we're all animals now, rutting, humping, sweating. Ben's neck tastes like salt, Roland's fingers dig into my hips, and my body matches Roland thrust for thrust, unable to stop myself from enjoying every inch of him.

I look down, savoring the messy state of Ben, just as his jaw tenses and his eyes roll back. Swears drip from Ben's clenched teeth as Roland begins jerking him furiously; I can feel the back of his hand and Ben's leaking tip bump repeatedly against my belly. The sight of him makes my pleasure climb to dangerous heights, and even though I *just* had an orgasm, suddenly I'm *there* again, right there, and ecstasy burns through my veins and makes my heart pump that much faster.

"Don't cum," Roland says, "not yet. I want to enjoy this a little longer."

I can't tell if he's talking to me—or Ben—but we both struggle to obey. My thighs quiver as I feel myself approaching the precipice for the second time, and I try to distract myself with Ben's mouth. We kiss sloppily, needy, hot tongues sliding and sucking with frustrated desperation. I slip my hand over Ben's, and his fingers lace with mine. We're tangled together, just as much as Roland and I are, my

161

pleasure, pain, delicious agony, all connected to his—if Ben loses it, *I'm* going to lose it, too, and I know it's the same for him because he makes a noise in my mouth that's half a growl, half a whimper.

"*Please*," I finally beg for the both of us when I can't possibly take any more, my lips still brushing against Ben's. I *have* to cum—I'll lose my mind if I don't.

"Yes," Roland pants at last, as his organ begins to throb inside of me. "Let go. Cum with me."

I cry out, and then Ben swallows my tongue in his mouth. My orgasm rips through me so ferociously, I want to cry, and I can't stop kissing Ben. I grip his fingers so tightly. Ben moans as I do, and the mattress shudders as his hips jerk off the bed, into Roland's hand, against my hip, and I feel him, the hot streams of him hitting my naked body, my stomach, my breasts. Roland drives me through every pulse before he lets go himself, shooting inside of me with a reverent murmur of my name and tiny kisses against the back of my neck, my shoulder blades, and my spine.

We collapse together, the three of us. I'm sticky with my men's little men, we're all slick with sweat, and we're panting, trying to catch our breath. Roland props himself over me so he doesn't crush me between them, but I live for this, the warmth of the two of them, our combined, blissful post-sex glow.

"We should get married every day," Ben murmurs finally.

"At least twice a week, I'd say," Roland agrees, and we all laugh.

We get more comfortable—Roland lies down on the bed, and I wiggle in between them. Ben spoons me and his hand rests at my belly—always protecting and watching over the little life in there. Roland looks me in the eyes, his own gaze violet and vibrant. He cups the back of my head and says seriously, "I love you, wife."

I grin like an idiot. "I love you, husband."

Then Roland reaches beyond me and slips his fingers through Ben's hair. "I love you, too, husband," Roland says.

"I love you, prat," Ben replies. I cover my mouth to laugh, and Ben bites my shoulder, then murmurs, his voice a honey-rich purr that sends a shudder through me, "And you, kitten."

"Meow," I say, because he knows—because this is our strange little language, our strange little world, where nothing makes sense, but it doesn't matter because there's just *so much love*, pure, hot, unconditional love.

I belong to them, and they belong to me, and each other. Forever. I wasn't sure what—if anything—would change after the ceremony, but I feel a subtle but real shift. Especially in Ben, whose biggest fear was always that he would be left in the dust.

He doesn't have to be afraid anymore. He's relaxed. Playful. *Silly.*

And all three of us are closer for it.

"Do you hear that?" Ben says after a moment soaking in silence.

"Hear what?"

"The ocean."

"You're like a bloody human conch shell," Roland yawns. "You can hear the ocean anywhere."

"Shh. Quiet. You can hear it if you're quiet."

I strain to listen. I can hear Roland's breaths grow deeper beside me. I can hear the low whir of the fan over us.

And then I hear it. From the open window, a soft breeze washes in, carrying the sounds of the ocean with it. I close my eyes and imagine foam-capped swells crashing against the cliffs below. Over and over, an unending rhyme, the ocean and the cliffs and the moon all orchestrating together this one, beautiful sound.

I fall asleep to the serene hush, our three bodies so tangled together we make one, our hearts beating in time.

28

BEN

SIX YEARS LATER

Something isn't right.

My eyes fly open. It's still dark—our bedroom is swathed in midnight-blue light. It's quiet. Roland and Rory lie in bed beside me, still deep in sleep, their chests rising and falling rhythmically.

So why do I have this nagging feeling of dread?

Silently, I climb out of bed. I slip on my trousers and exit the room. I nod to the guards outside and step down the hall, to the kids' room. When I open the door, I see the robin-eggshell-blue wallpaper. A full bookshelf, a wall of stuffed animals, a chest overflowing with toy trains, plastic boats, dragons, and monsters. Two empty beds.

No kids.

A shadow crosses my chest, and my heart picks up an extra beat. I move quickly down the halls, checking the usual suspects—the library, birds in the tearoom. My pulse doesn't stop pounding until I reach the kitchen.

There they are. Of course. Cleaning off a plate of blueberry scones, their small feet kicking at the table.

Alex, our six-year-old, notices me first. He's a dark-haired, lanky young boy—quiet, contemplative, and far too serious for his age. When he sees me, he almost drops his scone.

"We weren't doing anything wrong, sir," he defends quickly. "Ama had a nightmare."

For every bit that Alex is responsible and thoughtful, Ama is not. The little blonde is enjoying every second of her terrible twos, and when she sees me, the waterworks suddenly turn on, as though reliving the nightmare all over again. She lifts her fingers (stained with blueberry), her sky-blue eyes on me, bottom lip trembling, and cries, *"Dadadadadada."*

My shoulders sag. Unfortunately, I'm also a sucker for *dada*. I cave and lift her against my chest, where she sniffles her little crocodile tears into my shoulder. She's a warm, soft weight on me, and my heart calms.

"Good morning, sir," Miss Thompson says, shuffling around the kitchen.

"Miss Thompson. I don't suppose you had anything to do with this."

"Well, I couldn't sleep much myself and they were scampering around, and I thought, I need someone to taste the scones before I bake the lot of them for breakfast." She's not sorry for the rush of energy this sugary midnight snack is going to give them. Everyone at the palace—including Miss Thompson—loves spoiling them.

"Who forgot to invite us to the party?" A voice comes from behind me.

I turn to see Roland and Rory—wearing their bed head, robes, and amused grins. Ama, who is a complete traitor and a glutton for attention, reaches for Roland now and wails, "Dadadada!"

"She had a nightmare," I inform him as I pass her over.

Roland gasps dramatically and holds her up in front of his face. "A nightmare! What was it about?"

"Um…" She sniffs and her eyes flicker around, trying to concoct a memory. "Monster…"

"Oh no. The breakfast monster? Did he force you to eat your veggies?"

"Uh-huh…"

Meanwhile, Rory takes Ama's seat and picks at the scones with Alex. "Did you leave any for the rest of us, buddy?"

"You can have this one, Mummy," he says and hands over his half-devoured scone.

She grins and wipes some blueberry crumbs from his mouth before giving him a kiss. "You are the sweetest, you know that? What do you say we try to go back to bed?"

He nods and leaps off the stool, taking his mother's hand. "Thank you, Miss Thompson."

"Come back anytime! Keep this old woman company," she remarks.

I mouth a *thank you* to her, and she just gives me a knowing smile. Roland carries Ama, Alex walks beside Rory, and I slip my fingers through the little boy's hair, mussing it.

Of all the roles I've playing my life—brother, bodyguard, boyfriend—none have felt as right as *father*. The second they were born, Alex and Ama rearranged my whole world. They're my priority, my job, and my greatest accomplishment.

I lost my purpose for some time, but I found it again with these two.

So did Roland and Rory. Just when I didn't think I could love them more, I saw them transform into *Mummy* and *Dada* and my heart tripled in size.

We corral the kids back to their bedroom. They rinse out their mouths, then both scamper to the reading corner. It's a cushioned part of the room with large pillows stuffed against the walls next to their bookshelf, and it's big enough to fit our family of five. The adults sit, Alex takes his mom's lap, and bossy Ama has us all wrapped around her finger as she pulls a handful of books from the shelf, takes her time choosing the right one, and finally forces it into Roland's hands.

"Paddington Bear? Again?" Roland asks.

"Yep," Ama declares and plops herself into my lap. She's a daddy's girl—doesn't matter *which* daddy, as long as she's climbing all over one of us. She snuggles up on my chest and grabs her favorite toy—a snowy-white stuffed otter, a Christmas gift from her favorite uncle Oscar—and holds it tight as her eyes expectantly fix on Roland.

Roland tells the story, but with blueberry sugar in them, they're still not tired. So Ama picks out another book (this one for Mummy to read), and then a third book (this one she gives to me to read). I must have the most boring, monotone reading voice of all, because by time I'm finished, *everyone* is asleep, even the adults.

I soak in this moment. I want this to last forever. Everyone's peaceful. Happy. My family is protected, safe, and loved.

Rory's head is slumped to the side, and I slip my fingers through her ginger hair and press a small kiss to her head. Her eyes slowly flutter open. "Let's put them to bed," I murmur in her ear.

She nods. Gently, she lifts Alex out of her lap. He's practically boneless in her arms, and she carries him to his bed. I scoop Ama out of Roland's arms. Her tiny eyebrows knit, and she wraps her arms around my neck, clinging like a tiny koala. I carry her to her bed, adorned with daisy-patterned blankets, and tuck her in. She doesn't settle down, however, until I place her otter back in her arms. Then she's out like a light, clinging the softie. I tuck her long blonde hair away from her face.

I feel arms wind around my middle. Rory presses a small kiss to my back. "How did we make such beautiful babies?" she murmurs.

"Beats me."

I squeeze her arm. My heart is full.

"Let's wake our third child," she says and untangles herself from me when I nod in agreement.

Roland is in a deep sleep, slumped against the wall, book in his lap. Rory plucks a toy cat from the array of stuffed animals and taps its button nose against Roland's.

He blinks awake, then snorts on a laugh. "Good morning, kitten."

Rory puts her finger to her lips to hush him, motioning to the sleeping children. I extend a hand and Roland takes it and gets to his feet before the three of us quietly leave them to sleep on.

I pause in the doorway, though. I can't seem to tear myself away. They have a small nightlight plugged in, and I can see both of our kids in their respective beds. Tiny heads on fluffy pillows, their chests rising and falling in deep sleep.

I love these children. I love our family. Nothing has ever felt more right—or more perfect.

"Ben." I glance up to see Rory. She's halfway down the hall already, her fingers entangled in Roland's, and she's got that mischievous look in her eyes. "Are you joining us?"

The grin of hers makes my heart skip a beat.

"Always," I say.

I close the door and follow Rory and Roland to our bedroom. We stay up well past our bedtime, kissing and loving until our three hearts beat in the same, single rhythm. When we finally settle down, their body heat warms me. Roland's arm wraps around me, and Rory's lips press against the ring on my finger.

My children are safe and sound. My loves are tangled against me. And everything feels right. Finally, sleep begins to take me.

I've found my purpose. And I'll never lose it again.

THE END

DEAREST READER

Thank you for reading my novel, The Royal's Baby! These characters are near and dear to my heart and I'm so grateful that you've joined me on this wild journey with them. Don't forget to show your love for this passionate throuple by **spreading the word** to your friends and **writing a review!**

* * *

What do Rory, Roland and Ben do when their children become teenagers? Find out when you sign up for my newsletter and receive a completely **FREE bonus book** featuring the whole family!

* * *

Let's take it back to the start...

Did you miss the first time Rory met Ben and Roland? Get your copy of **The Royal's Pet**, with all its red hot passion, pent-up longing, and more than a dash of adventure.

ABOUT THE AUTHOR

The average day in the life of Adora Crooks involves sobbing about fictional characters, spoiling her nutty mutt, and watching Dr. Phil with her beloved. Adora lives off of coffee, chocolate, and book reviews. She lives in New Orleans and daydreams about dirty romances with happy every afters.

Don't forget: Bada$$ Babes Read Romance. Sign up for my newsletter to get exclusive deals on Adora Crooks stories, including ARCS and upcoming releases. Read on, my friends.

https://adoracrooksbooks.com/

ALSO BY ADORA CROOKS

MMF Ménage Romance

The Royal's Love (Complete Series)

When Rory's one-night-stand with the prince of England accidentally goes viral, Rory is pretty certain her life can't get any weirder. Add a brooding bodyguard, a meddling mother, and a plot to overthrow the throne, and, yeah. It just got weirder.

Truth or Dare (The Complete Duet)

At 18, Kenzi lost her v-card to her two best friends. Then came the fall out. She ran. Far. Twelve years later, her son is sick. The only two doctors that can save him are Jason and Donovan...the two men she swore never to see again.

All I Want For Christmas is Them

When Naomi goes out to a holiday-themed concert with her boyfriend, Otto, the last thing she expects is to end up in bed with Otto and his handsome best friend. But Otto is keeping a secret that may ruin more than Christmas...

Mr. Hollywood's Secret

Eric North is a leading man with a big secret—his live-in boyfriend, Nico. When Eric's agent sets him up with a fake fiancée, sparks fly between all three of them.

M/F Steamy Romance

Doctor All-Nighter

He's the playboy doctor next door. She's just trying to study. When a one-night-stand leads to a positive pregnancy test, they make a deal: they'll co-parent, as long as neither of them fall in love.

The Best Man Wins

She's a wedding planner with her career on the line. He's the best man determined to break up the engagement before the couple says their vows. It's a battle to the final "I do."

Protecting His Finch

He's an ex-military bodyguard to an elite mafia family. She's the family's ward. Will he risk everything to protect her?

HUNGRY FOR MORE?

Looking for more steamy bisexual romance? Keep reading for a sneak peak into my second chance romance, "The Bully's Dare", Part 1 of The Truth or Dare Duet...

THE BULLY'S DARE

KENZI

*H*e's the most beautiful boy I've ever seen.

Raven-black hair cut short around his ears. Sky-blue eyes underneath dark, pensive eyebrows. Lips that are just a little too big for his face. Dimples when he smiles.

He sticks out from the pack—but how could he not?—well over six feet tall and towering over everyone. His body is all lean muscle, and he shows it off under the summer sun, wearing nothing but black boardshorts. He's sitting on the deck of a fishing boat, perched on the rim, like it's a throne, surrounded by a cawing group of three boys and two girls, all in swimsuit attire and drinking wine coolers and shitty beer. They're blasting some Top 40, and it's echoing up and down the sleepy dock of Hannsett Island Marina.

At eighteen, he's been dropped into the body of a god, and it's clear from his posse and his confident grin that he's decided to wield his newfound power by the way of Dionysus—chaos, destruction, and *boys will be boys*.

And I'm bored enough to be entranced by his peacocking.

The only thing I'm working on is a tan, playing through my new Gwen Stefani album, and a rereading of *Little Women* (don't we all want to be Jo?).

I'm lying on a towel, Walkman by my side, sprawled out on the top of Four's sailboat, *Sweet Serenity*, which is currently tied up in a slip directly across from the party boat.

Four and Pearl are downstairs (or "below deck" as Four likes to correct me), and every now and then I can hear the blender roar as they down margaritas.

"Four" is short for "stepdad number four."

Which is all he will be, until stepdad number five.

It's not that I have anything against him—he taught me blackjack and he smokes Cuban cigars and he wears his hair in a long gray ponytail which he somehow pulls off. It's just that he's temporary, and there's no point in getting attached to something that won't be around for very long, anyway.

He owns both a beach house and a sailboat at Hannsett Island, an island off Long Island that you have to take a ferry in order to get to, which means that Pearl and I are basically stranded here for the summer. Pearl is my mom, but I haven't called her "mom" since I was five. I have a very vivid memory of her breaking me of the habit in Gabriel's Butchery on the Upper West Side, after I'd ruined her effort to pick up a man in a black tweed turtleneck along with her black-pepper ground salami. Apparently, it's hard to flirt when you have a little rug rat tugging on your dress begging for attention.

Getting out of the stink and hot asphalt of a New York City summer seemed like a great idea at the time. Until I realized that Pearl and Four were going to be the ones drinking and necking...while I got stuck with no friends, limited internet access, and skin that burns before it tans.

It would be better if I wasn't here. I get that. This is Pearl and Four's romantic getaway. I'm the annoying teenager who gets pissy when she's gone more than twenty-four hours without her Myspace account.

My captivity is made only marginally better by the eye candy in slip 12A. I glance over the top of my book. Raven-

Hair has got his legs splayed out, leaning back on his elbows, a posture that says *I own this room and everyone in it*. His friends address him as "King," and I can't tell yet if that's his name or if that's just his Holier Than Thou title.

God save us from the cockiness of a teenage boy.

I don't usually go gaga for jocks—they're too often assholes to girls like me, who got curvier once puberty hit. But there's something about his swagger that goes right between my legs. Maybe they grow boys differently in Long Island. Something in the water?

Or maybe it's just me. Nearly eighteen, never been kissed, hormones rocketing through me, making me boy-crazy, making me more of an *Amy* than a *Jo*.

King's boat is a tall motorboat with the words *Healing Touch* scrawled in gold cursive along the back. The engine is going now, gurgling, and it looks like they're getting ready to set off, even though I don't see any adults on board. Are they even old enough to drive that thing? And aren't they all at least semi-buzzed?

The water, I've learned, is lawless.

Curious, I move a headphone off my ear so I can snoop.

The dock boy unhooks the boat from the dock, untangling the lines and tossing them into the boat. Two more boys (obviously part of the party crew) come down the dock with a cooler between them.

"Get over here!" one of the girls shouts from the boat. "Or we'll leave you!"

I watch as the boys comically scramble over the side of the boat, carting the goods over first before tumbling in. Just as the final jock makes his landing, he puts his hand on the dock boy's chest. "Thanks, Dick Boy," I hear him sneer before giving the kid a shove. He goes tumbling backward and hits the water—much to the delight of everyone on board, who breaks into laughter.

Oh, *hell* no. I leap to my feet and throw a single barbed insult: "Assholes!"

It lands straight between the eyes of King, who—*now*—suddenly notices me. His eyes meet mine. They're way, way too blue to be real. His gaze feels like a bolt of lightning striking down my spine. It's hitting 90 degrees right now, yet my nipples are knots.

He gives me a cocky half-grin and shrugs a single shoulder as if to say, *Whoops*.

I feel the heat rise up my neck. Jerk.

The *Healing Touch* glugs as it leaves the slip, and every teenager on board hoots and hollers as they go further out to sea. I hope a kraken swallows them whole, honestly.

I leave my Walkman and book behind and leap from the edge of the sailboat to the wooden dock. The sun-charred slabs are stingingly hot underneath my bare feet, but I ignore the pain and crouch down to the edge to extend my hand.

"Need a hand?" I ask as the dock boy swims to the edge of the dock.

"I've got it," he grumbles, but as he scrabbles at the edge to get his footing, it's clear he *doesn't* have it. He takes my arm, and together we pull him up. His uniform—a white polo shirt with a small lighthouse stitched into the chest pocket and khaki pants—is soaked through. I pick a piece of seaweed from his shoulder, and he grimaces about it.

"Those guys are a bag of dicks," I tell him.

"Yeah," he says. "You don't know the half of it."

"Can I get you anything? A towel?"

"I'll live. The clothes aren't the problem." He's got these soft chestnut irises, and they meet my gaze for the first time. "You want to know the real tragedy?"

"Always."

He reaches into his pocket and pulls out a neatly rolled joint, now soaked and limp.

"RIP," he says.

I hold up a finger. "Hold on."

Why, yes. I have tricks up my sleeve. I reach into my bikini, where I've stashed away my one vice from Four and Pearl: a rolled joint and a lighter. For the moments I really need to escape.

For the first time, Dock Boy smiles. "Hello, new best friend."

"You can call me Kenzi."

* * *

DOCK BOY'S real name is Donovan. His real age is nineteen. I haven't discovered his real hair color yet, but I know it's not black because he keeps having to towel off his neck when the dark hair dye drips down around his ears.

Hannsett Island Marina is a self-contained ecosystem, complete with its own restaurant (the Blue Heron, accessible by the public) and a slew of private facilities: a general store, a private pool, a communal shower/restroom/locker room, and a laundry room.

There are only two sets of washers and dryers in the laundry room. Donovan sits on one of the washers, I sit on the fold-out table, and we pass my joint back and forth as his clothes tumble dry.

He's wearing only his boxers, but they look enough like a bathing suit that it's somehow not obscene. Doesn't keep me from admiring his body, though. He's lean, not quite stacked like the jocks, but I like the softness of him. He's kept on this thick leather-woven bracelet and a simple chain necklace with a ring on it.

"Promise ring?" I ask and point to it.

He frowns at that. "My mom's wedding ring."

"Divorced?"

"Deceased."

"I'm sorry."

He shrugs, and that's the end of that conversation.

I get it. I have things that *were* my dad's, sort of. Pearl kept his record player and a few tattered albums. I play them sometimes, but only because I like music, not because I liked him. He died when I was just a kid, and the memories I have aren't great ones, so we never had the kind of connection that inspired me to carry around any of his trinkets.

My head is a little hazy, and I swish my legs under the table. I feel small, but not in a bad way. The comfort of careless innocence. "So why do those guys hate you?"

Donovan thins his lips. He taps ash off onto the quarter slot. "I'm a loser. I'm gay. I don't have a yacht or a summer house. Take your pick."

"That's fucked-up. Have you told anyone about it?"

Donovan's eyes sharpen. "*Who*? No one cares. Jason King and his crew of idiots basically run this island."

King. That clicks. "Jason King...is that the tall one?"

"Tall, blue-eyed, and beautiful? That's the one. He's a rare breed of island native. Have you visited the Lighthouse Medical Center yet?"

"Nope, and from the sound of it, I don't want to."

"Good call. It's Hannsett Island's pride and joy, though. And the island's cash cow. Jason's dad owns it, which basically makes him richer than God. They have a mansion in the Dunes. Two boats. And a second house Upstate."

"All hail the Kings," I say which draws a little wry smile from Donovan. He holds out the joint in offering, but I shake my head. I'm already floating. An ant crawls over my knuckles, its tiny legs tickling, and I let it. I watch its perilous odyssey across the back of my hand and then back onto the table.

"Why are the pretty ones always jerks?" I wonder out loud.

I can feel Donovan looking at me. "You don't seem jerkish."

I stick my tongue out at him. He laughs.

* * *

...Find The Bully's Dare on Amazon to keep reading!

Printed in Great Britain
by Amazon

29501225R00108